Victor never wanted to come home, yet here he is. He's done the job that was asked of him, so he doesn't have a reason to stay, but he can't abandon the three untaught psychics he's met while rescuing Marcel. The fact that his ex-boyfriend can't take no for an answer doesn't matter, since Victor hopes Barton isn't aware of his presence.

Unfortunately, luck never works his way.

Tim wants to show his cousin that the mistakes he made when he was younger are far behind him. When Jerome agrees to hire him, he wants to make the best impression, and when they're hired to investigate the disappearance of several humans, he can both help find them and impress his cousin.

But things are never easy. The man who took Marcel is in business again, and this time, he's targeting humans. By fomenting the tensions between humans and shifters and using the right people, he's throwing suspicions in a direction that could be dangerous for Tim, Victor, and their friends.

Someone needs to find the people who have vanished before the unthinkable happens.

This book is a work of fiction. Names, characters, places, and incidents either are products of the author's imagination or are used fictitiously. Any resemblance to actual events or locales or persons, living or dead, is entirely coincidental.

It Takes a Psychic
Copyright © 2022 Catherine Lievens
ISBN: 978-1-4874-3500-4
Cover art by Angela Waters

Published by eXtasy Books Inc

Look for us online at:
www.eXtasybooks.com

It Takes a Psychic
It's a Psychic World 3

By

Catherine Lievens

CHAPTER ONE

Victor winced when the door of the room next to his slammed shut. He'd just been falling asleep, and the couple fighting next door had startled him awake. He'd hoped it wouldn't go on for too long, but instead, they'd been fighting for the past twenty minutes, and now all hopes of falling asleep again were gone.

Just like the woman who'd been fighting with her boyfriend, apparently.

Victor sighed and pushed himself into a sitting position. There wasn't much to see in his motel room. It wasn't home, just a place to lay his head and try to sleep, but he was having problems lately, even with that. It wasn't only that he was worried about everything that was happening, either. He didn't want to be here, but he had to be, and it was messing with him.

He rubbed his face with his hands, trying to shake the sleep off. He really needed to sleep, but since that wasn't going to happen, he might as well turn his attention to something else. The most pressing thing was that his funds were getting low, which meant he wouldn't be able to stay at the motel for much longer. He'd be glad to leave it behind, but at the same time, where would he go? The best thing to do would be to get an apartment, but that would mean living in the same town as Barton, and he wasn't ready to admit that was what he needed to do.

Being in the same town as Barton was never a good thing.

But there was no way out of it. The ghosts in town were

acting up because of Curt. If Victor wanted to help the PIs who'd already dealt with Curt once, he couldn't go anywhere. He was needed here, no matter how little he liked it. At least Barton didn't know he was in town. If he had, the man would already have been knocking on his door, telling Victor he was glad he'd come back to him and that they were going to be happy together.

Barton had always been delusional. What Barton wanted, Barton got, or at least, that was what he thought. He never understood that maybe Victor didn't want the same.

There was a reason they'd broken up, after all.

Victor got out of bed. He didn't want to stay here, thinking about Barton and about how much of a mess his life was. He didn't know anyone in town except for Barton, but he felt that if he asked for help, the PIs and the psychics would do what they could. That didn't make them friends, but maybe it could turn into friendship in time.

Victor wasn't sure he could allow that to happen. He hadn't trusted anyone since Barton except for his family, and he didn't know if he was ready or if he could. He supposed he'd find out soon enough.

His phone vibrating on the nightstand made him jump. His heart raced as he picked it up and peered at the screen, only relaxing when he saw his brother Olsen's name on the screen. It wasn't Barton. Victor's ex didn't know he was in town, and he wouldn't find out.

"Why are you calling me?" he asked as he answered.

"I'm feeling the brotherly love. What crawled up your ass and died?"

Victor found himself smiling even though there was nothing for him to smile about. "Brotherly love? What brotherly love?"

Olsen laughed. "That's what I was saying." His tone turned more serious. "How are you doing?"

"Can we not talk about it?"

Olsen snorted. "Fat chance of that. I'm worried about you. We all are. Just say the word, and we'll be there for you."

It was tempting to ask his brothers to come to his rescue, but Victor could deal with this on his own, and he could deal with Barton on his own, too.

As long as he stayed away from Barton's family. It wasn't enough that Barton was a rich asshole. His brother was the chief of police, and his best friend was the mayor. This city was all kinds of fucked up, which was probably one of the reasons Victor didn't feel comfortable here.

"I don't want you to come."

"We got that, but I'm not sure it's the best idea. You're dealing with something none of us have ever seen."

"Which is why I don't want you to come."

"So you can be in danger, but we can't?"

"It's not like I *want* to be in danger. I already am, and I won't leave these people on their own."

"Didn't you say they have two psychics?"

"They do, but they're untrained. Hell, one didn't even know he was a psychic until recently. What are they supposed to do? They don't know how to deal with ghosts, but I do. I'm the only one who can help them."

"Not true. You're the one helping them because they contacted you. They could have contacted anyone else, including Roslin or Donahue. If you don't want me to come, at least talk to them."

"I don't want them to be in danger any more than I want you to be," Victor pointed out.

"But we both know you're extra worried about me because I'm not a psychic. I get it. I just don't want you to have to face all of this on your own."

Victor thought about the people who worked at the PIs office. "I'm not alone."

"Fine, but are you with people you trust?"

"These people wouldn't hurt me."

"You don't *think* they would. You can't be sure, and even if they don't, they're not who you have to worry about. Have you found out more about what's going on with the ghosts over there?"

Olsen was an anomaly in their family because he was the only one who couldn't see ghosts. Being psychics was the family business except for Olsen, but that didn't mean he wasn't involved in it. All his life, he'd lived with people who talked to people he couldn't see. He was used to its nuttiness, and even though he couldn't help with ghosts, there was plenty he could do.

Victor still didn't want to involve him, or any of his other brothers, for that matter. "I think that adding more people to the mix will only make things worse," he said. "It's already a mess."

"Which is one more reason you should ask for help. I'm sure these people mean well, but you were the one who said their psychics are untrained. What are they going to be able to do to help you?"

"I'm training them."

"That's great. Is it going to be enough?"

Victor was pretty sure the answer to that was no, but what choice did he have?

Curt was still in town, hiding somewhere, no doubt plotting his next move. Whatever the shifter was planning wouldn't be good, which meant that Victor and the people who had contacted him for help would be the first defense for the humans who lived here. If Victor left, where would that leave them? They had two psychics, but they were untrained, even though Victor was trying to work with them. It took time to be able to control ghosts and to learn to call to them or send them away, and that was without whatever magic Curt was no doubt planning on using. From what they'd learned, Curt's girlfriend wasn't just a psychic but also a magic user. That complicated things in a way Victor hadn't expected, and he'd feel guilty if he left and something happened.

And something *would* happen. They just didn't know when or what, but eventually, Curt would try again, and Victor suspected he'd continue using ghosts. He had it in his mind that he could use a ghost army, and while Victor wasn't sure how useful those ghosts would be, it was true they could create mayhem or even hurt people. Usually, only the strongest ghosts could do something like that, but with what Curt and his girlfriend were doing, Victor wouldn't put it past them to create an army of ghosts who could do damage.

And Victor was right in the middle of it.

Olsen sighed on the other side of the phone. "Promise me you'll be careful."

"I will be, and if I need help, I'll call." Because Victor wasn't sure he'd be able to do this on his own, and if he couldn't, he'd have to call his brothers.

He couldn't put himself or anyone else in danger just because he was stubborn. He cared about his brothers, and he didn't want them to be involved because he was terrified of what could happen to them, but they were adult men, and they'd make a decision once he explained what was going on.

He knew they'd come. That was what they did as a family.

Tim made his way down the hallway, carrying a tray with two teacups on it. He could already hear the sound of his grandmother's television blaring in her room, and while it hurt his ears, it also made him smile. He'd have to knock extra hard for her to hear him.

A small table stood by the door of his grandma's room. He set down the tray and raised his fist to knock on the door. The table had been put here for this purpose. His grandmother was getting older, and even though she'd never admit it, she was having trouble with her hearing. No matter how many times Tim or anyone else begged her to see the healer, she refused, because she insisted there was nothing wrong with her except old age. That might be true, but it didn't mean the healer couldn't help her.

Tim wasn't surprised when she didn't answer the first time he knocked or even the second. By the third, he decided to risk it and open the door. He just hoped he wouldn't see anything that would traumatize him.

It wouldn't be the first time his grandma watched TV naked.

"Grandma?" he asked as he opened the door. He closed his eyes, just in case.

For a moment, nothing happened. Then the volume of the TV lowered. "Tim?" Tim's grandma asked.

"Are you dressed?"

She huffed. "You watch TV naked one time, and everyone makes a big deal out of it. I don't understand. These are my rooms. I can do what I want here, can't I?"

Tim opened his eyes. His grandma was sitting in her favorite armchair, the remote control in her hand. She was glaring at him, but that didn't make her less adorable. She was wearing her favorite purple skirt, black shoes, and a white shirt. Her short gray hair framed her wrinkled face, and while she looked like an adorable grandmother—and she was one—there was a fire in her that Tim hoped would never fade.

He leaned back to grab the tray, then walked into the room. "I agree that you can do whatever you want in your rooms, but you can't complain that I don't want to look until I'm sure you're dressed."

"Fine. I won't complain about it then. What did you bring me?"

He put the tray on the table next to her armchair. "Some tea and a couple of your favorite cookies."

"I was just getting hungry. Are you having tea with me?"

"If you want me to." Tim had expected the request, which was why there was a second cup on the tray.

He sat on the couch by the armchair, relieved when she turned down the volume of the TV completely. She didn't turn it off, but she never seemed to. When Tim asked her why she wanted the TV on at all times, she said it made her feel like she had company. It had made him feel guilty that he didn't spend as much time with his grandmother as he should, especially considering her age. She'd kick his ass if he mentioned that she was getting older, but that didn't change the fact that she was.

"You always spoil me," she said as she took a bite of cookie. "Now, what do you have to tell me about the clan? Your mother refuses to gossip, and your father wouldn't know good gossip if it hit him in the head. Who's having sex with who?"

Tim knew his grandmother, which was why he'd waited to take a sip of his tea. He'd have spat it out all over her if he hadn't. "You know I don't listen to that kind of stuff."

She grunted. "Maybe you should, at least for your old grandmother who barely leaves her rooms."

"You barely leave your rooms because you don't want to deal with everyone. If you wanted to, you would."

She waved Tim's words away. "People are so annoying these days. Now, tell me about them. Actually, why don't you tell me about the new guy? Your mother mentioned him, but she refused to give me any information. I think she was afraid I'd go find him, which is ridiculous. Why would I go find him when I could have someone tell him to come to me?"

Tim tried to imagine York talking to his grandmother. The guy was terrified of everyone in the clan, which made sense, considering the situation, but what would he think of Tim's grandmother? Even though she was a dragon shifter, she wasn't scary, but she could talk anyone's ears off.

"Have you tried getting him to visit you?" he asked, curious about the answer.

"Not yet. I wanted to find out more about him first."

"There's not much to say, unfortunately."

Tim's grandmother frowned. "How can that be? He's been with the clan for several days now."

It was more like several weeks, but he didn't say that out loud. "He's pretty much kept to himself. I think he's afraid of what the clan will do to him if he doesn't."

"Elijah wouldn't hurt a fly."

"We both know that, but York isn't one of us. Considering what he's done, I think it makes sense that he's afraid we'll punish him."

"Then you should go to him and reassure him that we won't. He's part of the clan now, isn't he?"

"I don't know. You'd have to ask Elijah about that."

"Maybe I will. Now, why don't you go to York and spend some time with him?"

"I'm having tea with you."

Tim's grandmother clicked her tongue. "Fine. We'll finish our tea, and then you'll find him. That boy needs friends, and there's no one better than you."

Her words warmed Tim's chest. Some people in his family had a bad opinion of him for something he'd done when he was younger. He understood where they came from, but he was trying to atone and make them see he'd changed. His grandmother had never stopped loving him or treating him the way she was now. Whatever he did, she still loved him, and she always would.

That unconditional love made him think of York. From what little York had said, he didn't have a family. He'd only had his brother, and he'd lost him in a car accident. That was why he'd agreed to work with Curt, and when he'd realized that Curt was up to something nefarious, he'd tried to back out. It had been too late, though, and while Tim was convinced York hadn't meant to hurt anyone, not everyone in their little group agreed. Maybe York needed to know that Jerome was an asshole to everyone, including Tim, who was his cousin.

Since he'd promised, Tim headed to York's room once he was done with his grandma. The door was closed, and Tim quickly knocked, hoping York would open. He didn't care that York had done something wrong. As long as he wasn't planning on hurting anyone else on purpose, he was a good guy in Tim's book. He'd done something stupid, but who wouldn't to get back someone they loved?

The door slowly creaked open, and York peeked out. His eyes widened, and Tim was pretty sure that if he could have gotten away with it without seeming rude, he would have slammed the door closed again.

Tim beamed at York. "Hi," he said.

York blinked. "Hi." He sounded much more hesitant. "Is there anything I can help you with?"

"I was just wondering what you were up to. Do you want any company?" Tim had decided to treat York as if he were one of his friends. Maybe in time it would become the truth, and in the meantime, it would hopefully help York feel like he was part of the clan.

They had a few clan members who weren't dragons, although most of those people were married to dragons. York didn't have such a relationship with anyone as far as Tim knew, which he suspected didn't help York feel like he was home.

"Why are you offering?" York asked in a soft voice. "You know what I did. I don't understand why you're treating me like this."

"Like what?"

"Like I deserve your friendship."

"As far as I'm concerned, you do. You did something stupid, but you did it because you wanted your brother back. Besides, as far as I'm concerned, everyone does stupid things when they're young. Now that you're finished with it, you can focus on the rest of your life, right?"

"Everyone here is so weirdly nice to me," York blurted out.

Tim grinned, and when York opened his door wider, stepped into the room. "And you haven't seen anything. Trust me. If you think we're weird already, you'll think we're downright nuts once you've been with us for a few months."

And hopefully, he would still be here then. York didn't have anyone else or anywhere to go, and Tim wanted the clan to become his family.

It was a good family to be a part of.

CHAPTER TWO

The waiting area was empty when Victor pushed open the door of the PI business. He could hear voices somewhere, so he knew someone was there.

He hesitated. Should he go back and try to find Lindsey and Will, or should he wait here until someone noticed him? Everyone was probably busy, but Victor had checked in with Lindsey before coming, and Lindsey hadn't said anything about him and Will not having time to see Victor.

Victor hesitated for so long that Lindsey found him. He was walking past the waiting area, but he paused and smiled at Victor when he noticed him. "What are you doing standing there?"

"I wasn't sure if I would be welcome deeper in the office."

"You could have come to the break room. Everyone's busy, but Will knows you're coming. I'm sure he's almost done."

Victor nodded and followed Lindsey to the break room. He didn't miss the fact that both Will and Jerome had clients in their offices, which struck him as odd. "You weren't kidding when you said they were busy," he said.

Lindsey grimaced. "We've been getting a lot of clients. It's almost too much for us to keep up with. It's gotten to the point that Jerome is thinking about finding help, and I think he would have already if he'd known who to ask."

"What about his cousin or Marcel's friend?" Victor remembered them from when they'd worked together to get to Marcel. Surely Jerome trusted them? Even if Jerome didn't want to ask his brother to help, considering what Marcel had gone

11

through recently, there had to be someone else.

"Don't mention Tim in front of Jerome."

"Why not?" They'd been a bit awkward around each other, but their relationship hadn't struck Victor as odd.

"Jerome doesn't like him very much. I disagree with that feeling, but there's nothing I can do about how Jerome feels."

"Family trouble?"

"Pretty much. I'm sure Jerome will get over it eventually, but I need to give him time. Maybe he could ask Marcel and Leo. It wouldn't be a bad idea, although we can't be sure they'd agree to help. They're busy."

"Isn't everyone?"

Lindsey laughed and gestured at Victor to sit down. "I suppose. Curt isn't making things easy on us with his ghosts."

Victor sat and leaned forward, interested in what Lindsey was saying. "You think that the reason you have so many clients are the ghosts?"

"I don't know. For the most part, people have been coming to us because someone they love has vanished. The thing is that instead of being supernatural creatures, it's humans coming. Usually, they already went to the police, but either they've refused to help, or if they tried, they haven't been able to do anything. I guess we're their last resort, and while I understand trying everything, I'm not sure how much help we'll be able to give these people."

Lindsey poured coffee into a mug and placed it in front of Victor, who nodded in thanks and wrapped his hands around it. It was warm, and he allowed his shoulders to relax.

"But you're trying," he said.

Lindsey poured himself a coffee, too, and leaned back against the counter. "We are. I know how hard it is on Jerome and Will not to be able to do anything to help these people, though. I don't want them to beat themselves up for it, but we also can't turn these people away and tell them there's nothing we can do for them. They're looking for a loved one, and they don't know what to do."

Unfortunately, Victor didn't have an answer for Lindsey. He wished he could help, but there was little he could do unless the vanished people were dead. The same went for Lindsey.

"I thought I saw you walking past," Will said as he walked into the break room.

"You were busy, so we didn't want to bother you," Lindsey answered. "Ready for our lesson?"

Will groaned and rubbed his forehead. "I know we have to do this, but I'm so freaking tired. Even when I'm not working, I'm thinking about work, and it's gotten to the point that Marcel has to drag me away from my files when I'm home."

Victor got to his feet. "It's probably best if we don't train today, then. You and Lindsey can both use some rest."

Will waved at him to sit back down. "We do, but this is important, too. Let's at least try."

"As long as you tell me if you're not up to it. You need to be focused to learn how to do this."

Will nodded and squared his shoulders. "I'll be focused. I can leave work behind for half an hour and focus on what you're saying."

Victor hoped that was the truth.

He leaned back, still holding his mug. "So, the two of you need to learn how to attract specific ghosts and repel them."

"I still don't understand why I'd want to attract a ghost," Will grumbled as he sat down at the table.

"It could be useful when it comes to your investigations. Instead of running around like Lindsey did during that first case with Jerome, he could have just tried calling the victim to himself."

Lindsey had told Victor about how he'd met Jerome in the first case they'd worked on together. He'd done a great job for a psychic with no training, and Victor couldn't wait to see how much better he'd get once he was done. Of course, learning was never over, but Victor could at least give Will and Lindsey the basics.

"You're not wrong," Will admitted. "So how do we do this?"

"It's all a question of focusing your ability. That's easier to do when you know who you want to talk to."

"So it doesn't work if you don't?" Lindsey asked.

"It can. You could also just focus on wanting to talk to a ghost and try to pull whichever of them is hanging around. It's a bit harder to do, because you don't have anything to focus on. It's much easier when you have a name, or better, a picture."

"What about repelling ghosts?" Will asked.

"That's even easier. If it's okay with you, we're going to try that today."

Will nodded and looked around. "How will you do it if there are no ghosts here?"

"I'll call a ghost and see if they cooperate." By now, it came easy to Victor. He'd been doing this most of his life, and it was like breathing.

His mother and father had wanted Victor and his brothers to know what they were doing when it came to ghosts. They'd taught them the basics when they were children, even to Olsen, who wasn't a psychic. It was one of the reasons Victor was so comfortable with ghosts—that and the fact that no one in his family had found him strange for talking to people they couldn't see. They could see the ghosts, too, which had made everything easier on Victor.

By now, Victor's senses were honed. He could identify ghosts and feel their presence, and when he reached out with his spooky sense—as Olsen called it—he quickly found a ghost. He gently pulled, giving her the opportunity to leave if she didn't want to talk to them, but she came.

When she appeared in the middle of the break room, she looked curious. She was a woman, possibly in her fifties, wearing a sweater and a pair of jeans.

"Hello," Victor said.

"Hello. How are you?"

"My name is Victor, and I'm a psychic. These are Lindsey and Will. I'm training them, and I was wondering if we could use you."

She cocked her head. "It depends. What are you planning on doing to me?"

"Just calling you to us, then trying to push you away. It won't hurt you."

"I suppose it's something to do. Death is much more boring than I expected it would be."

That made Victor chuckle. "We'll be happy to make it less boring for you, then."

He quickly talked Lindsey and Will through what they were supposed to do and how best to focus on pushing the woman away. Lindsey was already making friends with her, so now they knew her name was Melissa, that she'd left behind a husband and two daughters and a grandson. She visited them often, but sometimes it hurt too much not to be able to be part of their lives.

Neither Lindsey nor Will managed to repel Melissa the first time they tried. The only way to get it was to continue practicing, so Victor told them to do just that. He gave them pointers, but they knew the basics now, so there wasn't much he could do for them. His thoughts drifted, and like always lately, they settled on Curt.

What was the man doing? How could Victor and the others stop him? Was there anything they could do, or was it a lost cause?

Victor hoped that wouldn't be the case, but he'd never

found himself in this kind of situation. He was terrified he wouldn't be enough, because if he wasn't, who would be? Who would step in and help Jerome, Marcel, and the others?

Tim was nervous when he and Marcel reached the office. "You're sure Jerome won't mind?" he asked.

"Why should he?"

"He doesn't like me."

"He tolerates you. He's not going to kick you out."

Tim wasn't too sure about that. He wanted to show his cousin that he could do good things and stay on the right side of the road, but he wasn't sure Jerome would give him a chance. He'd said he would, but so far, Jerome had kept his distance, and every time Tim was with him, he looked at him as if he thought Tim was going to steal his wallet or his phone. It hurt, but it hadn't deterred Tim yet. He was stubborn enough to stick it out.

Or at least, he hoped so.

Marcel walked into the PI office as if he belonged there, and Tim supposed he did. There was no one in the waiting room, but they could hear voices deeper in the office, so they headed that way. Jerome was talking with a crying woman, so they didn't bother them. Tim had something to say to Jerome, but now clearly wasn't the right moment to do it.

"You did good," Tim heard someone say.

He thought he recognized Victor's voice, and it brought a smile to his lips. Before he and Marcel could reach the break room, the door to Jerome's office opened behind them. They both paused, and Jerome stepped out, the crying woman right behind him.

"Let me walk Mrs. Robinson to the door, and I'll be with you," he told Marcel and Tim.

Tim had to resist the urge to run away. Instead of doing

that, he nodded curtly.

"You'll be fine," Marcel said as he guided him toward Jerome's office with a hand on his arm.

"He's going to say no."

"Probably at least once. You know him. He's grumpy and gruff, but he'll give you a chance."

"What if he doesn't?"

"Then you'll find someone else to work for. They need you, though."

"They could just hire anyone good with computers."

"Even if that were true, they wouldn't. Jerome doesn't easily trust people."

"I doubt he trusts me."

Marcel pushed Tim into one of the chairs in front of Jerome's desk. "Maybe, but he trusts strangers even less. No matter what he thinks of you, you're family."

Maybe, but Tim was a family member with a history of stealing. Jerome had been vocal about how much he disliked that and distrusted Tim.

"What are the two of you doing here?" Jerome asked as he walked back into his office.

He looked much more tired than he had the last time Tim had seen him. It made him wonder what was going on, but he was afraid to ask.

"Tim has a proposition for you," Marcel said.

Jerome's eyes narrowed. "Why would I want to listen to it?"

Tim cleared his throat. "Why wouldn't you? Just give me a few minutes."

"Do it for me," Marcel said.

Tim saw the moment Jerome gave in. He was doing it for his brother, but then, he'd do pretty much anything for Marcel.

Marcel was still too thin after what had been done to him.

He'd been kept in a magical coma for weeks while his life energy was being sucked out to help raise more ghosts and give them a strength no ghost should have. Luckily, they'd managed to get to him in time, and he was doing fine now, but they'd all been terrified for him for a while. It was obvious Jerome was still scared for his brother, and that was probably the only reason he gestured at Tim to explain himself.

Tim nodded. "You know I'm good with computers."

"I know you're good at stealing with computers."

Tim groaned. "Yes, I know I did something stupid. You don't have to bring it up every time we talk to each other."

"Why shouldn't I? Someone should tell you how stupid you were."

"I already know I was stupid. But what I did doesn't change the fact that I'm good with computers. I think I could help you."

Jerome frowned and leaned closer. "How?"

"Just like you needed Lindsey to help with the ghost aspect of your job, I believe you need me to deal with the computer side."

"Will and I can do research on our own."

"I'm sure you can, but it's not easy. Besides, I have more experience than you with computers, and I probably can get the same result in much less time. Considering everything that's happening, I think you should give me a chance to show you I can be trusted and that I can help you."

Jerome stared at him for so long that Tim was sure he'd say no. He wouldn't be surprised, and he prepared himself for rejection. It would hurt, but he wouldn't give up on his attempts to show his cousin he wasn't the same kid who'd played Robin Hood on his computer.

"And why are you here?" Jerome asked Marcel.

"For support," he said easily. "Tim knows you don't like him, and I wanted to make sure you gave him a chance."

Jerome rubbed his eyes. "It's not that I don't like you, Tim."

"You just don't trust me."

Jerome looked apologetic, although only a little. "Considering what you did, you can't be surprised."

"I'm not, but I want to show you I can do better. I *have* been doing better. You're the only one who can't see it, and I want that to change."

"Why?"

"Because we're cousins. We're family, and I don't want to lose you when it's not necessary." York had lost his brother, and he was destroyed. There was nothing he could do about it, but there was something Tim could do about Jerome and his rejection.

Jerome stared for a moment longer. Tim steeled himself, waiting, barely breathing.

"Fine," Jerome finally said.

Tim blinked at him. "Fine?"

"You can work with Will and me, although I'll have to talk to Will about it."

"He'll say yes," Marcel said.

Jerome glared at him before turning his attention back to Tim. "As I said, I'll have to talk to Will, and this is on a trial basis. I'll be keeping an eye on you, and if you do anything wrong, you'll be out the door so fast that you won't realize it until you're on the sidewalk."

Tim nodded eagerly. "That's fine. I promise I won't do anything stupid."

"I hope you won't. Now, which cases do you think you can help us with?"

"All of them. I can help with the ghosts and the normal cases, and anything that requires a computer. I can't promise I'll solve your cases, but I'll do everything I can to help you with them."

"It's fine. I already said you could help."

"You won't regret it."

"I hope I won't, but I guess we'll see."

Jerome still didn't trust Tim, but that was okay. Tim would show him he could be trusted, if it was the last thing he did. Now that Jerome was giving him this opportunity, he'd finally be able to do it. The fact that he'd also help people was a bonus, but that wasn't the main reason he'd wanted to do this. No, the main reason was to gain Jerome's trust, and Tim felt he'd finally taken the first step toward that.

"You did good," Victor said.

Will wrinkled his nose. "I don't know about that. I only managed to repel Melissa once."

"Which is one time more than you've been able to do it before. Trust me. You're great, and while it's going to take time and practice for you to get better, you have the basics. Now you can do things on your own."

"Does that mean you're leaving?" Lindsey asked.

He had an easier time than Will understanding what Victor was explaining, possibly because he'd always known he was a psychic. He'd never been trained, but he'd known he could see ghosts all his life, unlike Will. The fact that Will hadn't realized that some of the people he saw on a daily basis were ghosts baffled Victor, but he supposed that humans were great at burying their heads in the sand when it came to things they didn't want to face.

"I can't leave while Curt is still out there, doing who knows what," Victor said. "But I also can't continue living at the motel. I need an apartment." Even though the last thing Victor wanted to do was live in the same city as Barton, there was no way out of it. If he was going to help, he had to stay.

"We can help you find something," Lindsey offered. "What will you do for money, though?"

"I'm a consultant, and I have a good following. Usually, my clients find me through people I've worked for, and since I already worked here, it won't be a problem to find jobs."

"I'm glad to hear you're staying. Honestly, I was a little worried that Will and I would have to shoulder all of this ghost stuff."

"I wouldn't leave you alone with them."

"If you need anything, you can call either one of us," Will said as he got to his feet. "Now, if you'll excuse me, I probably have a long line of clients waiting for me."

"You work too hard," Lindsey said. "Both you and Jerome."

"What choice do we have? No one else is helping these people, and we can't kick them out."

It was clear it wasn't just because of the money. Will and Jerome wanted to help their clients, and they were pushing themselves to do so.

"I should probably go," Victor said, following Will's lead. "The two of you need to keep practicing. The more you do so, the easier it will be for you to control ghosts."

"Is that something we'll be able to do?" Will asked as they walked out of the break room into the hallway.

"Not in the way you're asking. What I meant is that you'll be able to control whether or not ghosts can bother you. Once you have that control, you'll even be able to go a while without seeing them. It's a matter of practice."

"I kind of wish I'd never found out I could see ghosts," Will said as they stopped next to his office door. "But on the other hand, I like helping people."

"You would do that even without being able to see ghosts, but I understand what you're saying."

Will gently patted Victor's shoulder. "Well, I have work to do. Feel free to come by anytime you want."

"Thank you." Maybe Victor would. It would be better than

staying in his hotel room listening to his neighbors fighting.

Will disappeared into his office just as the door to Jerome's office opened. Victor expected to see him, but instead, Tim came out.

Victor had met Tim when they'd been looking for Marcel. Tim was Marcel and Jerome's cousin, and while there was some bad blood between him and Jerome, everyone else had been happy to have his help. They probably wouldn't have found Marcel without him, and Victor had been impressed with his work.

He was also impressed with the way Tim looked.

Victor wasn't going to deny that. He liked Tim's personality, but also his appearance. His dark eyes always seemed to hold a hint of mischief, and while he was slight, he was also very obviously strong. The fact that he could turn into a giant dragon shouldn't be as appealing as it was, but Victor kind of wanted to ask him if he could shift for him. He'd never do something like that, but the thought was never far from his mind when he was with the man, and that never happened with any of the other dragon shifters Victor had met.

But instead of asking him to shift for him, Victor plastered a smile on his face and moved toward him. "Hello," he said.

Tim clearly hadn't seen Victor come closer, because he was startled so hard he took a step back and hit the wall. Victor winced, but he knew better than to reach for Tim. He didn't want the dragon shifter to hurt himself again.

"Victor!" Tim said. "What are you doing here? Not that you can't be here. I mean, I'm here, too."

Tim was a grown man, and he could kill Victor with barely a thought, yet he was also adorable. Victor didn't understand why Tim seemed so intimidated by him, but he wished he didn't. "I was working with Will and Lindsey," Victor explained.

"On the ghost thing?"

"On the ghost thing," Victor confirmed, smiling at how Tim was saying it. "What about you?"

"I was talking with my cousin. I offered Jerome to help with the computer side of things, and he said I could give it a try."

"That's good."

Tim bounced on the balls of his feet. "It really is. I never thought he'd trust me again after what I did, but maybe we're on the right path."

"Well, I'm happy for you."

Tim gave Victor a beaming smile. He was handsome even when he didn't smile, but when he was like this, he made Victor want to grab and kiss him.

Victor didn't think Tim was anything like Barton, but he couldn't help but think of his ex. He'd been hurt and betrayed when he'd left Barton, and he wasn't sure he was ready for anything new, especially not the kind of relationship he was sure Tim wanted. At the very least, he wasn't ready for the kind of relationship Tim deserved.

"Well, hello there," a male voice said.

Victor turned around, trying to identify the man. He didn't sound like anyone he knew, but he was sure the man was a ghost. He knew he was right when he saw the man standing behind Tim. He was leaning against the wall, looking with interest from Victor to Tim.

"Hello," Victor said.

Tim frowned, then looked around both of them. "You're not talking to me, are you?"

Victor shook his head. "I'm talking to the gentleman behind you."

Tim looked back, but he couldn't see anyone, since he wasn't psychic. "There's a ghost here?"

Victor nodded, then cocked his head to take a better look at the ghost. He looked familiar, but Victor was sure he'd never met him.

"I stay away from Tim for a few weeks, and he manages to bag a guy like you?" the ghost asked.

Victor blinked. "You know Tim?"

"Of course I do. He's my grandson."

Victor hadn't expected that, but he doubted Tim had, either. "My name is Victor."

The ghost gave him a little wave. "It's a pleasure to meet you. I'm Kenneth."

"I don't suppose Tim knows you're here?"

"I love that boy, but he doesn't have a psychic bone in his body. I've been following him for years."

Victor had to suppress a smile. "Do you want me to tell him?"

"Tell you what?" Tim asked.

"He's never had the best patience," Kenneth confided. "But he's entertaining to follow. His cousins are, too, and with so many handsome men around this office, I think I'll start spending more time here."

Victor didn't know what to make of Kenneth, but since the ghost didn't have a problem with him telling Tim about his presence, he turned to Tim. "I was just talking to your grandfather."

Tim's eyes widened. "My grandfather?"

"His name is Kenneth? He says he's been following you around because you're entertaining." Victor wasn't sure what to make of the *handsome men* remark, but he didn't want to out Kenneth to his grandson if the ghost didn't want him to.

"I'm entertaining?" Tim sounded like he didn't quite believe it.

Victor shrugged. "I'm just repeating what he said."

"I know. I just didn't expect my grandfather to follow me." Tim hesitated. "You think I could talk to him? I mean, could you help me talk to him?"

Victor knew it wasn't the brightest thing to do if he didn't want to risk developing feelings for Tim, but he found himself nodding anyway. "I'll help you."

Tim was stunned at the news that his grandfather had followed him around. He'd never met the man, so he hadn't expected something like that. His grandmother would be delighted to find out, and she'd have something to say to her husband—probably things Tim didn't want to hear.

Tim hadn't missed the fact that he wouldn't have known about his grandfather if Victor hadn't been with him. It was one more reason to keep the man close, but not the main reason Tim wanted that to happen.

Tim had so many questions that he didn't know where to start. He knew he could say them out loud so his grandfather would hear them, even though it was strange for him to speak to nothing. "When did he start following me around?"

Victor was silent for a moment. He stared at the spot in front of Tim, which made Tim feel better about talking in that direction. At least he hadn't been speaking to the wall.

"He says he started when you were a baby. He was surprised when your father married a human, and he was curious to see how you would come out." Victor chuckled. "Apparently, it's better than he expected."

Tim had no idea what that meant. He wanted to ask so many things, but he wasn't sure Victor wanted to be involved. He'd said he'd help, but was it fair to him, especially since Tim wasn't paying him? "Does he want me to tell my grandmother he's around?"

It was odd to have to wait for Victor to listen to someone Tim couldn't see, but Tim didn't have a problem with it, and besides, he enjoyed watching Victor in the meantime.

The man was as gorgeous as he'd been the first time Tim

had met him and all the times after that. He wasn't usually the kind of guy Tim went for, but he was much more interesting. It wasn't just the ghost thing, either. Victor's dark hair, dark clothes, and sparkling gray eyes made Tim want to know more about him. Victor was mysterious, but he was also nice and gentle, and Tim could see them becoming friends, maybe more.

"He says you can tell her if you want, but only if you think she'll take it well," Victor finally said. "He's been hanging around her room, too."

That wasn't something Tim wanted to think about. "He doesn't think she'd be happy to find out he's there?"

"He says that they didn't have time to talk about their death when they were together. She's lived a long life without him, and it wouldn't be fair to put this weight on her shoulders if you don't think she could take it."

"I think she can take pretty much anything, but I understand."

Tim's grandfather had died at the age of only forty-six. Tim's father had been twenty-one at the time, while Tim's grandmother had been only a few years younger than her husband. She'd lived half her life without him, so it made sense that Tim's grandfather might not want her to have to carry this weight. Tim thought she'd be happy to find out that he was still around, but he could be wrong. Maybe she hoped he'd gone to heaven or whatever she believed in. Maybe she'd be distraught if she found out that wasn't so. Hell, she could even be creeped out by the fact that her husband had been hanging around her for the past forty years.

"I'll think about it," he said. "But I know my father would be happy to know his father is still around."

"Kenneth says you can tell him." Victor looked back at the empty spot. "Yes, I can do that. Just let me know when you want to do it, and I'll make sure to be available."

"What's he saying?" Having to ask was kind of annoying, but Tim was grateful he wasn't a psychic. He'd seen what it did to Lindsey and Will, who weren't trained. He wouldn't have wished that on anyone, especially not on people he cared about. He wasn't sure he would have been able to deal with it, and it was good he didn't have to.

Victor smiled at him. "He wants me to go to the clan so he can talk to your father."

"Shouldn't you find out if my father will be okay with it first?"

"Kenneth wants me to try, so I will. I have no way to know how your father will take it, but I never find out until I talk to the people I need to contact."

Tim thought about it. "Honestly, I don't know how he'll react. He hardly ever talks about his father, but my grandfather died forty years ago. I'm sure he still thinks about his dad, and when he does talk about him, it's obvious he cared very much about him. I'm just not sure how he'd take it if he found out that his father has been hanging around him for the past forty years."

Victor laughed. "Your grandfather wants me to tell you that it's not like he's been staring at you and your father in private settings. He knows what privacy is, and besides, with so many people he cares about, he's been making the rounds."

It was good to know his grandfather hadn't been with him in the bathroom when he showered or something like that, and Tim felt kind of ashamed he'd thought it might be the case. But he'd never known his grandfather, so who knew how he was? Tim's grandmother certainly never had a problem barging into the bathroom when he was showering when she still went around the clan. If she had something to tell him, she just came in, scoffing when he scolded her for it.

Knowing her, he was kind of curious about what kind of man his grandfather was.

"What are the two of you doing there?" Jerome suddenly asked.

The sound of his voice so close when Tim hadn't heard him made him jump. He turned around, his eyes wide, an apology on his lips.

"Sorry," Victor said. "It was my fault. I noticed a ghost hanging around Tim, and I told him about it. We were talking with Kenneth."

Jerome frowned and looked from Victor to Tim. "Kenneth?"

"My grandfather," Tim said. "My grandmother Nancy's husband." He and Jerome were cousins because Jerome's father was Tim's mother's brother. They were both human, and they'd both married dragon shifters. Kenneth wasn't Jerome's grandfather, but Jerome had heard about him.

"Your grandfather is hanging around?" Jerome asked.

"I didn't know about it until now. I still wouldn't if Victor hadn't told me."

"Uh. Well, you can talk about your grandfather all you want, but not in my hallway. Besides, I'm sure Victor has better things to do. He's not here to help you talk to your grandfather or your dead cat."

Tim huffed. Did Jerome have to be so snarky? Tim understood his cousin didn't trust him, but that didn't mean he had to be an asshole.

"Oh, I don't mind," Victor said. "At the moment, I don't have much to do. I just had a lesson with Lindsey and Will, but now, I'm at a loss. Talking to ghosts is my everyday life, and it was entertaining to meet Kenneth."

Jerome narrowed his eyes. "Still, we have work to do, and this is an office."

Tim raised his hands. "I'm going." But he really hoped his cousin would stop treating him as if he were an undisciplined and annoying child.

He knew he'd done something stupid when he was younger. He'd never done it again, and he wanted to prove himself, but he was starting to wonder if Jerome would allow him to do so. Jerome was so bent on thinking that Tim was a fuck up and would be for the rest of his life that it seemed impossible for him to change his mind.

Not that Tim would stop trying. He wanted to be part of this, to help Jerome and the others defeat Curt. He wanted Jerome and everyone else to see him like a man who could be helpful, and he'd do whatever he could to make that happen. Tim wanted them to get along, and fighting with Jerome wouldn't help.

That was the main reason he kept his mouth shut even though he wanted to snap at his cousin. It was also why he walked down the hallway, heading toward the entrance. He wasn't sure where Marcel had ended up, but he'd find out. He was probably making out with Will in Will's office.

Victor chuckled, and when Tim turned to look at him, he realized Victor was still talking to his grandfather. He wanted to ask what the man was saying, but he didn't want to interrupt.

"I like your grandfather," Victor said. His eyes went unfocused again. "Thank you, Kenneth. And you're right. Jerome *is* very grumpy."

Tim found himself smiling. He didn't know what to think of his grandfather, but the man seemed more similar to Tim than Tim had expected.

CHAPTER THREE

V ictor looked around and wrinkled his nose. "It's . . ."
He wasn't sure how to finish that sentence. The apartment had walls, a front door, and windows, but that didn't mean it was a nice place.

"It could use some work," the landlord said gruffly. "But I can give it to you cheap."

Victor nodded, but he had no intention of renting this place. The only thing he wanted to do was run away screaming because he was pretty sure spiders were climbing all over him. He swore he could feel their little legs on his skin, making him shudder in horror.

The apartment consisted of a kitchen that held a table, two chairs, a couch, and a piece of furniture that should probably hold a TV. It was empty, and the surface was covered in a thick layer of dust that made Victor sneeze just by looking at it. There was also a tiny bedroom and the smallest bathroom Victor had ever seen. The ceilings were low, and in one of the corners of the kitchen, Victor could see water damage. Not that it was easy to see anything, considering how grimy the windows were.

"Cleaning is on you," the landlord continued. "But you won't find anything better in the area."

Victor was sure that was a lie. Couldn't the landlord have cleaned up a bit at the very least? He understood that some changes couldn't be easily made, like buying new cabinets since he counted three doors that hung askew, but a good cleaning could probably have made this place look at least

30

habitable. As it was, Victor wondered if he'd have to share the place with rats.

Considering the stench of mold, dust, and even urine, he wouldn't be surprised.

He forced a smile on his face. "I'll let you know," he told the landlord.

The man glared. "I already have another three people wanting to rent this place. If you want it, you have to take it."

"I'll let you know as soon as possible," Victor promised. He needed a shower, and he needed it now before the dust sank into his skin. And good Lord, was that a cockroach in the corner by the window?

Victor couldn't get out of there fast enough. The landlord was already opening his mouth, no doubt to tell Victor he needed to take the apartment now, but Victor didn't let him speak. He took a step back, stumbled over a cracked tile in the kitchen, and rushed out the door.

The rest of the apartment building was pretty much like the apartment itself. Victor didn't look around as he made his way to the entrance, eager to be gone. He noticed a couple of ghosts, but he didn't stop to talk to them. It wasn't just that he needed out of the building but also that he'd stopped talking to random ghosts he met in his everyday life. He wouldn't talk to strangers on the streets, so why do it with ghosts?

He stumbled out the front door, reaching for it to catch himself, then changing his mind when he saw it was as dirty as the rest of the place. He snatched his hand back with a grimace, took several steps away from the door, and allowed himself to lean against the brick wall. He took a deep breath, and even though it smelled of car exhausts and the city, it was better than what he'd breathed inside the building.

He thumped the back of his head against the wall. He needed an apartment, but he couldn't live here. Maybe he needed to call Will and Lindsey and ask them for help. Trying to do this on his own clearly wasn't giving him the result he needed, and he couldn't survive more visits to places like this one.

He was relieved for the distraction when his phone vibrated in his pocket. He quickly took it out and pushed away from the wall, eager to get to his car. Once he was back at the motel, he could grab a shower, but first, he'd answer this phone call from his brother.

"First Olsen, now you," he told Roslin. "What's going on? Do you miss me that much?"

"Yes, I'm calling because I miss you," Roslin said dryly.

"Oh, you're so sweet," Victor continued teasing.

He could practically hear his brother roll his eyes. "Where are you?" Roslin asked.

"Almost at my car. Why?"

There was a pause before Roslin spoke again. It was enough to make Victor anxious. He knew he'd been right when his brother said, "Barton called."

Victor tripped and almost fell on his face. "What?"

"You heard me. Barton called. He's looking for you."

"What did you tell him? Why did he call you?"

"Probably because he doesn't have your new number. I didn't give it to him, so don't worry about that."

"How can I not worry?"

"I know. He asked me where you were, and while I didn't tell him, I'm afraid he'll find out in other ways. I remember how well connected he is. No one I know is talking, but someone will eventually, especially if he lets his wallet talk. Maybe you should move again."

It was tempting for Victor to jump in his car and drive out of town. "I can't abandon these people. They have a huge ghost problem on their hands, and it's only going to get worse." Victor hadn't seen many ghosts after what happened with Curt, but he doubted Curt had given up. Something was going to happen, and he suspected it would happen soon. He couldn't abandon his new friends, no matter how much he wanted to.

Roslin sighed. "I understand you want to help, but you might get hurt, and then you won't be able to help anyone."

Victor finally reached his car. He unlocked the door and slipped inside, taking a deep breath and relaxing at the familiar scent of cherry air freshener that surrounded him. He closed his eyes and leaned his head back against the headrest, trying to put his thoughts into order.

He wasn't surprised to find out Barton was trying to reach him. He'd expected that, just like he expected Barton to find him eventually.

"I'm being careful," he promised.

"I know. You don't want to see him after what happened, and you'll do anything you can to make sure you don't have to. He's influential and rich, though. That's going to make finding you easier."

"I'm safe."

"Just make sure not to end up somewhere alone with him. If you can, stay with your friends. Are you still staying at the motel?"

"For the moment. I'm looking for an apartment, but it's not going well."

There was a moment of silence before Roslin asked, "So you're planning on staying there indefinitely?"

"I don't know how long I'll be here, but I'm training two psychics, and I can't abandon them."

"I could come to help you. It would make it faster, which means you'd be out of there faster."

It was tempting to say yes. Victor wanted to see his brothers, and he wanted them to reassure him that Barton wouldn't find him. They couldn't do that, no matter how much Victor wished for it.

His family had never liked Barton, and now that Victor had taken several steps away from his ex, he could see why. Hell, he'd known why even before he'd broken up with Barton. He should have known better than getting involved with the older man, but he'd been blinded by the attention Barton gave him, and not just that. It was all over now, or he'd hoped it was. The fact that Barton was looking for him pointed toward the fact that maybe it wasn't.

"Really, Victor. What's going on there that you can't leave even though Barton is looking for you?" Roslin asked.

"I already told you they asked me to help them find a guy, right? A dragon shifter?"

"Yeah, but you haven't said much more after that except for the fact that you did find him."

"Well, he was kidnapped. There's a shifter here who wants to take over the world or something stupid like that, and he thinks he can do it by using ghosts. He's using his girlfriend, who's both a psychic and uses magic, to manipulate ghosts. He kidnapped shifters, used magic to suck out their life energies, and used it to raise more ghosts and make them more powerful."

"Shit. And that guy you were looking for is fine?"

"We found him in time, but several of the other shifters with him didn't make it. The guy, Curt, ran away, but we know he's going to try something else."

"Right. I understand why you want to stick around, although I'm even more worried about you now."

"I'm doing everything I can to be safe. Besides, at the moment, there's nothing much happening. Curt is probably plotting something somewhere, but for now, the only odd thing happening around here is people vanishing."

"And you don't think this Curt guy has something to do with it?"

Victor didn't have an answer to that question, but he

suspected his brother was right.

Whatever was happening, wherever these people ended up, he would have bet all his money that Curt was behind it.

York threw a bit of popcorn at Tim's head.

Tim ducked so it wouldn't hit him in the forehead, laughing as he did so. "What did I say?"

"I was *not* drooling over Leo!"

Tim laughed harder. "Okay, maybe not drooling, but you weren't discreet about the fact that you find him hot."

York's cheeks looked like they were about to burst into flame, they were so red. "He's just a good-looking guy."

Tim splayed a hand over his heart. "Aren't I a good-looking guy? Because you weren't looking at me that way."

York tried to burrow himself deeper into the pillows of his bed, but there was nowhere for him to go. He turned his attention back to the TV screen, but Tim doubted he was watching the movie they'd put on earlier.

It was good to see York coming out of his shell. It had taken some work on Tim's part, but York finally seemed to feel comfortable with him. At the very least, he was comfortable enough to ask Tim if he wanted to watch a movie in his room and to throw popcorn at him.

"It's okay if you like Leo," Tim said. "Although I don't know what you see in him. He reminds me a bit of my cousin Jerome, and considering how grumpy Jerome is, it's not a good thing."

"Leo isn't grumpy," York argued.

Tim arched a brow, which was enough to make York blush again.

"Okay, maybe he's a bit grumpy. That doesn't mean he's not sexy. Besides, this is pointless. It's not like he's ever going to look at me with anything but hatred."

That wiped the smile right off Tim's lips. "Why wouldn't he? You're cute, and you're a nice guy."

York stared down into the bowl of popcorn he was holding. "We both know that's not true. I kidnapped Leo's best friend, and I hurt him. Why would Leo give me a chance?"

"Why wouldn't he? Marcel isn't angry at you for what you did. Now if he never wanted to talk to you again, I'd understand. Leo, though? Why would he hold a grudge when Marcel doesn't?"

York shrugged. He was still too thin, and his shoulders were uncomfortably bony. He was getting better, although he was still eating all his meals in his room. Sometimes, Tim wondered if he was afraid that one of the dragons would eat him. He wanted to reassure York that if they decided to do so, it wouldn't be in a cannibal kind of way, but rather in a sexy way, but he wasn't sure that would make York feel better.

"Why did you do it?" he asked quietly.

York still didn't look at him. "You already know why."

"Not really. I remember you saying that Curt promised to help you get your brother back, but that's all I know. You don't have to talk to me if you don't want to, but I'd like to get to know you better."

York's gaze flickered to Tim's face. "Why?"

"Because I like you. I feel like we're becoming friends, and I want you to know I'm here for you if you need anything. I hope the same goes for you and that you'd be there for me if I need something."

"Why would you need anything from me?"

"There's no way to know. It could happen, though, and one can never have too many friends."

Having said that, Tim turned his attention back to the TV, but he kept an eye on York. He could see York slowly relax the longer Tim kept his mouth shut, and he wasn't surprised when, a few minutes later, York started talking.

"Cooper was five years older than me. I was always an odd child, but I didn't understand why people looked at me strangely. It took me a while to realize that they thought I was talking to myself when I was actually talking to ghosts. My parents tried to change me and make the psychic side of me disappear, and when they couldn't, they didn't take it well. My father especially got violent and tried to beat the psychic out of me."

Tim tightened his hands into fists. He wanted to find York's parents and beat the shit out of them, even though it wouldn't solve anything.

"As soon as Cooper turned eighteen, he left the house, and he took me with him. My parents were happy to get rid of me, so they didn't try to get me back. It wasn't easy, and I'm sure I gave Cooper more trouble than he wanted, but he never gave up on me. He found one job, then two, and at one point, he was working three jobs so that he could have enough money to feed me, buy me clothes, and give me what I needed. We were working things out, and it felt like we were finally settling down and making it work when a drunk driver didn't stop at a red light. My brother was crossing the road, and he didn't stand a chance. He was only twenty-two when he died. I was seventeen."

Tim's eyes burned. He didn't want York to think he pitied him, because that wasn't true. He was just so sad for both York and Cooper and for everything they could have had and everything they'd lost. It made sense now that York had been ready to do everything he could to get his brother back.

"After he died, I was alone. It wasn't long before I got kicked out of the apartment and ended up on the streets." York's voice was matter-of-fact, but what he was saying was anything but. "I worked odd jobs, just enough that I could earn money to feed myself. Sometimes, I managed to find an apartment for a few months, but it never lasted long. I was drifting, and I didn't know what to do without my brother. I kept hoping I'd see his ghost, but I never did."

"I'm sorry you lost him," Tim murmured. He couldn't even start to imagine how York had felt. He'd never lost anyone important to him, not the way York had.

"Thank you. I should have known better than to trust Curt. He found me at my lowest. I was living on the streets a few years ago, and I think he saw me talking to a ghost. He offered me food, some money, and a possible job. He said he wanted me to use my psychic abilities, and I was stupid enough to ask him if he could help me get my brother back. I didn't tell him everything I told you now, but I guess he could read me well enough that he knew how important that was to me. He promised he'd help me get Cooper back, and once he did, I wasn't going to say no."

"What happened when you realized what Curt was up to?"

"I knew Cooper wouldn't like it if he found out I hurt people to get him back, so I wanted to stop. I went to Curt and explained myself, and he changed. He wasn't a nice guy who wanted to help me anymore. He threatened me, and I knew he would kill me if I tried running away. It was tempting, but I wasn't the only one there, and it was easy to imagine him taking it out on the other people he tricked into helping him."

"Most people would have done what you did. Hell, Jerome would have done the same if it meant saving Marcel. He's still angry at you, but eventually, he'll realize that. Grief and hope can make you do things you normally wouldn't do." Tim wasn't sure it would be a good idea, but maybe it was time for York to leave the bedroom he'd been staying in since he'd arrived at the clan. It had become a safe place, and that was good, but there was more to life than four walls. "Why don't we go to the office?"

York's eyes widened. "Why would I want to go there?"

"Why not? We're still trying to find out what Curt is planning, and you could help us."

"I never really learned to use my powers. I just did what Curt told me to do."

"Then you can train with Will and Lindsey. They have a psychic who's teaching them how to use their ability, and I'm sure he'll want to teach you, too, once we explain the situation." It was just the kind of guy Victor was, and it was one of the reasons Tim liked him so much.

York looked cautiously optimistic. "You think he would?"

"I *know* he would, but why don't we go ask him?" That way, Tim would see Victor again. He was running out of excuses to do that, so he was glad York was giving him a new one.

When Victor was convinced Barton had followed him in the grocery store, he knew it was time to distract himself and do something that would put him in contact with others. He'd been obsessing over Barton since his brother had called him, and it wasn't good for his mental health. He needed a distraction, and the best way to get one was to head to the office. Maybe Lindsey and Will would want to ask him more questions, or he could even help them train. As long as he had something to do that meant he wouldn't be thinking about Barton, he didn't care what it was.

He dropped the stuff he'd bought at the grocery store into the trunk of his car and climbed into the driver's seat. It was a short drive to the office, and he was lucky enough to find a parking spot right in front. He wasn't surprised to see two people waiting in the waiting area, and since he didn't know what to tell them, he ducked his head and quickly walked past them and into the hallway. He'd been told to go straight to the break room when he came around, so that was what he did.

When he stepped into the room, he blinked at the man sitting at the table. York had both his hands wrapped around a steaming mug of coffee, and he looked like he'd rather be anywhere but here. When he saw Victor, he seemed almost afraid.

"Hi," Victor said.

"Hi," York answered, his voice slightly trembling. "I came with Tim. He said it would be okay for me to be here."

Victor smiled. "It's not my office, but it's perfectly fine as far as I'm concerned. It's good to see you."

"It is?" York sounded surprised.

Victor supposed he understood where York was coming from. After all, he'd been the one who kidnapped Marcel and sucked out his life energy. He hadn't done it because he wanted to, but still. It couldn't be easy for him to see the people who'd been looking for Marcel or Marcel himself. York had taken it hard, and he felt guilty about what he'd done.

"You don't strike me as someone who would do what you've done because you take pleasure in it or because it would help you gain something you want."

"I did it to get my brother back."

"But when you agreed to go along with what Curt was asking, you didn't know what exactly he wanted you to do, right? He promised he'd help you with your brother, and you said yes."

York nodded. "And when I found out what he wanted me to do, I tried to stop."

"See? That's what I meant. If you'd been like Curt, you wouldn't even have hesitated. Instead, you tried to help Marcel, and in the end, you did."

"I was stupid to think I could get Cooper back."

Victor could only imagine how much it would hurt if he lost one of his brothers. He understood why York had been ready to do pretty much anything to get his back.

He cautiously sat at the table in front of York. He didn't want to spook the man, and York already looked frightened enough. He was ready to bolt, and Victor didn't want to startle him.

"You have nothing to be sorry about," Victor said slowly.

York shook his head. "I should do more. I know Curt is still out there, probably planning something else. I feel like I need to stop him to atone for what I did to Marcel."

"You can't stop him on your own—but maybe you could give me and the others all the information you can remember. Like, we know Curt works with his girlfriend, who's psychic and uses magic, but did he have other accomplices?"

York frowned. "He didn't usually come around except to beat us up, but I think he was with a guy once."

Victor's stomach churned. "Would you happen to know the guy's name? Was it maybe Barton?" Because knowing Barton, Victor wouldn't be surprised if his ex were involved. All that mattered to Barton was money and power, which Curt wanted, too. If Curt could give Barton what he wanted, Barton wouldn't hesitate to work with him.

Victor had been thinking about this for a while, but he hadn't allowed himself to believe it could be a possibility. With Barton looking for him, though, he couldn't afford to ignore it anymore.

York shook his head. "I've never heard that name, but I suppose it's possible. It's not like Curt talked to me or the others about his plans. We didn't even know why we were taking the shifters' life energy. We did it because we were scared of Curt and his girlfriend."

Victor hadn't expected York to give him a positive answer, but he'd had to try. He wished he still had pictures of Barton, but he'd gotten rid of the few he had, and Barton was camera-shy—or at least that was what he'd always claimed. "Don't worry about it. It's just something I was wondering."

"Is this Barton someone you know?"

"He's someone I wish I didn't know, but yes. I have a history with him, and I wondered if maybe, he was involved."

"And it wouldn't be a good thing if he were, I take it."

"Definitely not. Hopefully, he has nothing to do with it." Victor supposed they'd find out soon enough.

He and York talked for a bit longer, and when Victor got to his feet to go to the bathroom, York looked more relaxed. He even smiled at Victor when Victor said he'd be right back, and Victor carried the smile out of the room.

Tim was leaning against the wall by the open door, doing something on his phone. He looked up when he heard Victor and quickly put his phone away. "Hey. I heard you and York talking, and I didn't want to bother you."

"So you stayed out here? You could have come in."

Tim smiled easily, and when he did, he illuminated the room—or in this case, the hallway. "I know, but it was good to see York talking to someone who wasn't me. I've been making friends with him, and he's slowly coming out of his shell, but he's still terrified someone here is going to hurt him. I can't exactly blame him when my cousin hates my guts, but I wanted him to see that it's just Jerome. Even Marcel forgave him, and I want him to forgive himself."

Victor looked back through the open door. York's head was bent as he looked at his phone. "I don't know if that's going to be easy."

"I'm sure it won't be." Tim hesitated. "Are you okay?"

It took Victor a moment to realize why Tim was asking. "You heard me asking York about Barton."

"I didn't mean to listen in on your conversation, but there are people in the waiting area, and the offices are all occupied. The break room is really the only place where I could go, and since I didn't want to bother you and York, I stayed out here."

"It's fine. And yes, I'm okay."

"You don't look like you are." Tim leaned forward, reaching for Victor's arm, but he snatched his hand back before touching him.

Victor wanted to tell him it was okay and that he could touch him wherever he wanted, but the words were stuck in his throat.

Tim was nothing like Barton. He'd already shown that to Victor, but Victor was still terrified. What if he gave Tim his heart the way he had with Barton, and Tim stomped all over it? What if Victor got hurt even more?

Logically, Victor knew that wouldn't happen, but his heart wasn't okay with them trying, at least not yet. Barton was still ruining Victor's life, even though he wasn't in it anymore.

Victor hated him for that.

Tim was attracted to Victor. There was no denying that, and Tim didn't want to deny it anyway. He wanted to comfort Victor and ask who that Barton guy was, but he was afraid it wouldn't be welcome. Victor was obviously freaked out, even though he was trying hard not to let it show, and Tim never wanted to hurt him or anyone else. He wanted Victor to feel safe with him, but he was starting to realize it would be a slow process, just like it was with York. Victor might not be as obviously hurt as York was, but that didn't mean he wasn't hurt as well.

Victor sucked in a breath. "You're right. I'm not okay, but I don't want to talk about Barton. I don't think anyone ever wants to talk about their exes, right?" Victor attempted a laugh, but it didn't sound right.

Tim wanted nothing more than to drag the man into his arms, but now that he knew Victor's ex had something to do with this, he was afraid of what the guy might have done to

Victor. It was better to keep his hands to himself, even though Tim suspected that it wouldn't be as unwelcome as he'd first thought.

Victor was still staring at Tim's hand, so Tim slowly reached out for him. He quickly squeezed Victor's hand before letting go, and he hoped it was enough to let Victor remember he wasn't alone. "I know you're alone here in town, and I want you to know that you can call me if you need anything," he said.

Victor smiled. This time, it was more natural, which Tim hoped was a sign that Victor was relaxing. "Do you offer that to everyone?" Victor asked.

"Pretty much. I told York the same thing, and I mean it. If either of you needs anything, I want you to call me."

"You're a good person, Tim."

Tim shrugged. "I don't think I'm better than anyone else."

"I doubt your cousin would have offered me what you just offered."

Tim chuckled. "That's because Jerome's a dickhead and only likes Lindsey. Honestly, I'm still not sure how the guy managed to seduce him. I also don't understand how he can stand Jerome, but I suppose love is blind and all that."

"I think there's more to your cousin than you think. Jerome probably only lets a few select people see that."

Tim grunted. He wanted to be one of those people, but his relationship with Jerome needed work, which wasn't easy when Jerome barely spoke to him. Tim was stubborn, though. In the end, he'd get what he wanted. "Do you need anything?" he asked Victor.

Victor shook his head. "No, thank you. I was just headed to the bathroom."

"Oh. Sorry to bother you, then."

To Tim's surprise, Victor hesitantly pressed a hand against Tim's chest. "You didn't bother me. I don't think you ever could, even if you tried."

Victor's cheeks flushed and he took his hand away, but it was too late. He'd already stolen Tim's heart, even though he didn't know it.

Victor rushed down the hallway toward the bathroom, and Tim watched him go. He didn't know what to make of what had just happened, but hopefully, it meant Victor was interested in him. He certainly was interested in Victor, and while the situation wasn't the best for starting a relationship, Tim wanted to see where things could go between him and Victor. Maybe they'd find love in between fighting ghosts and an asshole shifter who wanted to conquer the world.

Tim could always hope.

CHAPTER FOUR

The office was cramped, but Tim supposed it could have been worse. Jerome could have put him to work in the bathroom or maybe in the alley behind the office. As it was, Tim had to share with Lindsey, but that was okay. It was much better than having to share with Jerome.

He'd been surprised when Jerome had shown him to the office on his first day of work with his cousin. It had been obvious that someone had brought in a second desk, because there was barely space for two of them, but somehow, Jerome and Will had made it work. It had made Tim feel welcome, but he hadn't said anything about it. He didn't want his cousin to think he was trying to butter him up or something like that.

He was looking for information on one of the cases Jerome had given him a file for when a quick knock on the door made him look up. Jerome stood there, looking like he'd rather be anywhere but here, and Tim held his breath, wondering what was up.

"Can you come to my office?" Jerome asked.

The bottom of Tim's stomach dropped. Had his cousin already decided to fire him? "Of course. What do you need me for?"

"It's for a client."

Tim relaxed. His cousin wasn't firing him. He wanted help with a case, which was why Tim was here.

Tim got to his feet, snatched his laptop from the desk, a pen, and a notebook, followed Jerome's trail in the hallway, then to Jerome's office.

"As I was explaining, we have a computer specialist," Jerome said. "This is Timothy James. He'll sit with us and take notes, if you don't mind. For now, he's the best person for the job."

Timothy quickly sat down in the empty chair in front of Jerome's desk. The client was in the other one, and he stared at Tim as Tim set up his stuff.

The man had to be in his late thirties. His brown hair was starting to go white on the temples, and it was made more obvious by the fact that it looked like it hadn't seen a brush in a while. It wasn't that the man was unkempt, just that it looked like he'd had other things to focus on than brushing his hair.

"Tim, this is Brandon Fitzgerald. His wife Marlene disappeared a few weeks ago."

So this was one of the vanished cases Will and Jerome had been working on. Tim didn't know if he'd be able to find Marlene, but he'd do his best. "I'm sorry for what happened to you," he told Mr. Fitzgerald.

"At least you're willing to do something about it. The only thing the police told me was that my wife was an adult and that she had the right to disappear if she wanted to. No matter how many times I tell them she'd never have left our children and me, they don't seem to care." Mr. Fitzgerald's voice trembled. "I know you can't make promises. But I'm desperate, and I need someone to look into this. If she's—if she's not coming back, I need to know, and so do my children."

"Why don't you talk us through what happened?" Jerome asked.

It was odd to hear him like this. As far as Tim had seen, the only times Jerome was soft and gentle were with Lindsey. Yet he was talking to Mr. Fitzgerald as if he were afraid the man would break.

It was a distinct possibility. The man looked fragile, and as he started talking, his voice broke several times. "She's a nurse, and she volunteers for several organizations that help homeless people. She wasn't at work the evening she disappeared, but rather, working with one of those. It wasn't the first time she did it, and while I never went with her, I know she distributed meals and care packages to the homeless. I don't know what happened. She left for her volunteer work in the afternoon, and she should have come back around midnight, but she never did."

"When did you start getting worried?" Jerome asked.

Tim was taking notes. He wasn't sure what would be important in this case, so he wanted to get as much as possible down. Every little detail could help him in his search for Marlene Fitzgerald.

"She was late sometimes, but I always waited up for her. When she wasn't home by one, I called her supervisor. He'd been getting worried, too. They're supposed to work in pairs, but with so much work to do, sometimes, they separate. He'd noticed a fight between two men, and he'd stepped away from her. By the time he was done breaking up the fight, she was nowhere to be seen. When he couldn't find her anywhere, he told me to call the cops. That's what I did, but they weren't of any help. They told me she should probably be home by the morning and contact them again if she wasn't."

Mr. Fitzgerald swallowed loudly. He looked like he was about to cry, and Jerome reached for a pack of tissues on his desk. He slid it toward the man, who took one of them with a grateful nod. He wiped his eyes, then crumbled the tissue in his hand.

"The next morning, she still wasn't home. Once I took my children to school, I went to the station and explained what had happened. They told me it was too soon to open a case and that she'd probably come back. It was no use telling them that she would never leave us like that and that she wouldn't abandon her job. They told me to come back a few days later, and I did. They did file a report that time, but they told me that she was an adult and could do whatever she wanted. They won't believe me when I tell them that she's not gone because she wanted to go. Someone took her, and I don't know how to get her back."

Jerome asked more questions about the area where Marlene had been when she disappeared and her job. Tim wrote everything down, but his brain was already working. He wanted to see if there were security cameras in the area where Marlene had been working. If she'd been kidnapped, he might be able to find her on the feed somewhere.

He opened his computer, entered the password, and used the information Mr. Fitzgerald had given him to start his research. He lost himself in camera feeds and information about Marlene Fitzgerald. Like her husband had said, she was a nurse and volunteered with an organization that helped homeless people. Nothing in her life hinted that she might want to dump her husband, her kids, and her job and disappear. It was still a possibility, but Tim didn't consider it for more than a few moments. It didn't matter that Marlene was an adult or that she might have decided to vanish. Tim hoped that was the case because it would mean she was fine, but he suspected it wasn't and that her story wouldn't have a happy ending.

"Tim?" a voice asked right next to Tim's ear.

He startled, almost throwing his computer at the voice. When he peered up, it was to find Will standing next to him, looking down at him with a frown.

Tim blinked and looked around the office. Mr. Fitzgerald was gone, but Jerome was leaning back in his chair behind his desk.

"Where's Mr. Fitzgerald?" Tim asked.

"He left about fifteen minutes ago," Jerome said. "He said goodbye to you, but you only grunted in answer."

Tim rubbed his face with his hand. "I'm sorry."

"No need to apologize. You already started looking for his wife, right?"

Tim nodded. "And I think I found something." He'd watched the feed several times, mostly because he hadn't been sure what he was seeing. He still wondered if maybe he was missing something, but he wanted to show Will and Jerome.

He turned his computer so both Jerome and Will could see the screen. "Once Mr. Fitzgerald told us where his wife was working that night, I pulled up security feeds from cameras around the area. It's not exactly legal, Jerome, but I'm not stealing anything."

Jerome waved Tim's words away. His focus was on the screen as Tim started the video. "This is her. She's talking with someone, possibly a homeless man, although I can't be a hundred percent sure. I haven't identified him yet. Once she's done with him, she turns toward this alley. I think she sees something or someone, because she grabs another meal and goes that way. She never comes out."

"How is that possible?" Will asked.

"I don't know, especially because this alley is closed off at the other end. There would have been no way for her to walk out from there, which meant she'd have to come back. I don't know how she left without the camera seeing her." He turned the computer toward himself again. "And it's not the only thing I found. She's not the only one who's vanished this way. People have started talking on social media, finding each other. They lost people, in some cases their wife, their husband, adult children, or a parent. These people just vanished into thin air, and they haven't been found so far. There's a pattern here, although I'm not sure what it is yet."

Jerome's expression was grim. "Curt?"

"Right now, I don't know anything more than what I just told you."

"I think it's time for us to call Victor again. We may need to talk to ghosts, and if we can, to the ghost of one of these people who've disappeared."

Tim hoped Marlene wasn't dead, but he agreed with Jerome's grim expression. What would be the odds that she hadn't already been killed?

Victor was relieved when his phone rang and he saw Jerome's name on the screen. He needed a distraction, and he needed it as soon as possible. He'd been obsessing over Barton, and it had never done him any good.

"Hello?"

"Victor? This is Jerome Allais."

"I know. What can I do for you?"

"It would be great if you could come to the office. We have another client whose wife has vanished, and we're starting to wonder if these people are dead. It would be great if you could try contacting them."

"You think it has something to do with Curt?"

"I don't know, but I don't believe in coincidences. I'll eat my pen if he has nothing to do with these disappearances."

Victor suspected he wouldn't have to. He hadn't been here since the beginning of the thing with Curt, but people had started to vanish the first time, too. The difference was that then, it had been supernatural creatures. This time, it was humans, and while they could be useful, they were less powerful than shifters. They didn't have the same amount of life energy, and if Curt was using humans the way he'd used shifters before, it meant he was killing them.

That, in turn, meant Victor would have someone to talk to,

even though he wished he wouldn't.

"I'll be there as soon as possible."

"Thank you. I'm calling York and Marcel, too."

"You think they'll be able to help?"

"At the moment, we don't have anything. These people have vanished into thin air, and we're unable to find them. We need all the help we can get."

"And you have mine. I'll see you soon."

Victor quickly threw on a pair of dark jeans and boots and grabbed his jacket. He was out of his motel room only five minutes later, just in time to hear his neighbors start fighting again. He was glad he wouldn't have to listen to them this time around, although he wished it were for a better reason. His job was to talk to dead people, but it wasn't easy, especially when these people had died recently.

Ghosts sometimes didn't realize they were dead. Even when they saw their body, they tried convincing themselves that it was all a dream or maybe a joke someone was playing on them. For some, seeing their body and understanding they were dead was so shocking that they didn't speak for days or sometimes weeks. Victor wanted to help all of them, but the problem was that he still wasn't sure why some people became ghosts and others didn't.

Some psychics thought it was because the people who stayed behind as ghosts had something they still needed to do, but Victor didn't believe that. He'd met people who were looking for a dead family member because that person still had something to tell them or do, and he'd met ghosts who had no reason why they were left behind. They could have forgotten that they meant to do something and hadn't had the time before dying, but things weren't that easy, in Victor's opinion.

It also didn't have to do with the way these people died. He'd met ghosts of people who had died peacefully in their sleep, and he'd been unable to find ghosts of people who had been violently killed. He didn't think anyone had ever studied that kind of thing, and he kind of wanted to, but he also enjoyed eating and having a roof over his head, which meant he didn't have the time to do that. Besides, there was something more important for him to do at the moment.

He had to look for a parking spot when he reached the office. Several cars were parked in front of it, which wasn't surprising, considering how many people had to be at the office at the moment. Victor found himself hoping Tim would be there, too. He wanted to see the dragon again, and while he didn't need an excuse to do so, he felt uncomfortable contacting him just so they could spend time talking. He and Tim weren't together, and even though he was pretty sure Tim was interested in him, Victor didn't know what to do with it. He wasn't ready, and at the moment, he wasn't sure he ever would be.

The front door opened before Victor reached it. Will smiled at him and gestured him inside, and Victor followed him. "You're the last one to arrive," Will said.

"I'm sorry. I came as quickly as I could."

"Not a problem. We're in the break room, since that's where the coffee is."

The break room was crammed with people. Jerome and Will were there, and, like Jerome had mentioned, so were Marcel and York. Lindsey was present, of course, as was Tim. Leo was also there, which Victor hadn't expected, but maybe he should have. Leo had been there to save Marcel, too, after all.

"Sorry I made you wait," Victor said as he slid into a chair next to Tim's. Tim beamed at him, and Victor found himself smiling back.

"We were just talking about what we think is happening," Marcel said. "I believe that Curt is behind all of this. It can't be a coincidence. He lost all the shifters he was using as his personal life energy battery, and now, he needs more."

"But these people are human," Leo pointed out. "Could he use them?"

They all turned to look at Victor. He tapped his fingertips onto the table, his thoughts going back to what he'd been thinking earlier. "He could be using humans," he said. "They don't have the same amount of life energy, but they're easier to control than shifters and probably easier to kidnap. How many people have vanished?"

"Fifteen in the last month," Tim said. "I'm not sure if all of them are related to this case, but it's a possibility."

"That would make sense, because, if Curt is using humans, he needs more of them to get the same amount of life energy. There's also the problem that since humans have less of it, they'll die much faster than a shifter would, especially a dragon shifter. You need a lot of life energy to be able to shift into such a big animal."

"Would they be using the same spells they used on me?" Marcel asked.

"I couldn't tell you that. I know a bit about magic, but I don't have one bit of power in me, so I never learned. If we need to ask someone these questions, we have to find a person who knows what they're talking about."

"And where do we find that?" Tim asked.

"We need a mage. The problem is that I don't know anyone here in town." Not anyone who wasn't linked to Barton, anyway.

When Victor had run out of the city, he'd left most of his things behind, including the contacts he'd had. Even if he hadn't, he wouldn't want to use them. Those people were like Barton. They didn't let anything stop them from getting what they wanted, which was one of the reasons Victor thought Barton might be involved in this.

His phone vibrated in his pocket, and he took it out to check if it was one of his brothers calling or maybe his parents. His stomach dropped when he saw Barton's name on the screen.

He wanted to delete the number or even block it, but Barton would keep calling even if he did. He knew not to answer this way, but it still meant he had to see Barton's name on the screen more often than he wished he did.

"Problems?" Jerome asked.

Victor looked up to tell him he was fine, but the words died on his lips.

The room had been crammed full of people before, but it was even worse now. Ghosts surrounded Victor and the others, and not one of them looked friendly.

Victor paled so quickly and so much that Tim wondered if he was about to faint. The look of horror on Victor's face didn't help, and Tim reached for Victor's arm, squeezing it.

"Victor?"

"What the fuck?" Will muttered.

When Tim looked up, he realized both Lindsey and Will were looking around the way Victor was. Since the three of them and York were the only ones who could see ghosts, Tim was ready to bet that ghosts had appeared in the room.

"Lindsey?" Jerome asked, taking his boyfriend's hand.

"It's ghosts. They suddenly appeared, and they're everywhere in the room."

A whimper made Tim look at York. York appeared as if he was trying to become one with the chair he was sitting in. His eyes were wide, and his gaze bounced from one side of the room to another. His chest fell and rose quickly with his breathing, and he looked like he was on the verge of a panic attack.

Thankfully, Tim didn't have to worry about him, because Leo stepped in. Tim didn't understand why, since Leo hadn't made a secret of the fact that he disliked York, but for some reason, Leo scooted his chair closer to York's and wrapped an arm around his shoulders. The gesture was enough to jolt York out of whatever state he'd been, and he sank against Leo's side.

Tim turned his focus back on Victor. "Do you recognize any of these ghosts?"

Victor shook his head. "No, but it doesn't mean anything. I count thirteen, no, wait, fourteen. They're all just standing there and staring."

Tim hated the fact that he couldn't see the ghosts. He also couldn't do anything, not to protect the people in the room, not to help Victor and the other psychics. Victor was freaking out, which meant something was wrong. Tim doubted so many ghosts often gathered in a room and stared at people, and considering what they were working on, he wondered if maybe these people were the people who had vanished.

"And they're not doing anything?" Jerome asked.

"Not that I can see," Victor answered.

Tim wasn't surprised when Victor got to his feet. He did the same, wanting to be close to Victor in case something happened. It was ridiculous, since he wouldn't be able to do anything to help, but it made him feel better.

Victor turned toward the wall. From what Tim could see, there was nothing there, but he knew that wasn't the case.

"Hello," Victor said. "My name is Victor."

Tim waited, hoping the ghost Victor was talking to was answering. He wasn't surprised when Victor shook his head, though. "Hello?" Victor insisted.

Everyone felt like they held their breath, but nothing changed.

"None of them are answering," Victor said. "They're not

doing anything except staring. I don't understand if it's an intimidation tactic or if there's something more to it. There's no way for me to be sure whether Curt sent these ghosts."

"It's the only explanation," Jerome muttered.

"I agree. I don't see who else could have sent them, but if they don't answer my questions, I don't see a way to find out."

"Will the four of you be able to focus on the meeting with the ghosts here?"

Victor nodded, then looked at the other three psychics. They did the same, even York, who looked terrified.

"Let's continue, then," Jerome declared.

Victor took his seat back next to Tim. Tim leaned closer, wanting to reassure him. "You think they'll attack?"

"It's impossible to know. I hope not, though."

Tim nodded and patted Victor's arm. Victor seemed bemused, but he didn't tell Tim to cut it out, so Tim thought it had been welcomed.

He certainly hoped so.

"Is there anything we can do to find these people?" Jerome asked.

"I'll continue looking into this," Tim answered. "But I don't think there's anything more I can do. These people just vanished from alleys and buildings. One woman was in her apartment when she was taken. Her neighbors never saw her leave, yet, the next morning, she was gone."

"How do you think Curt is taking them?" Leo asked.

He still had his arm wrapped around York's shoulders, and York seemed almost at peace there. It was odd to see the expression on his face, but if this was what helped him, Tim was glad he was getting it. He was still surprised, but it was none of his business, as long as Leo treated York right.

"If this is Curt's doing, he has to be working with someone who can use magic," Victor said. "We already know his girlfriend can, but I doubt she'd be able to do this on her own. Besides, since they're taking humans now, they'll need more magic power. I don't think one person is doing all of this, which means Curt is probably working with more than one mage."

Tim rubbed his face. "Is there any way to identify the mages he could be working with? Like, if you need a mage, how do you find them? Is there a directory?"

Victor shook his head. "It's a word-of-mouth job, just like being a psychic. We don't advertise. We work with clients, and those clients tell their friends about us."

"So there's no way to know who Curt is working with."

Victor hesitated, then shook his head. "Not for sure. I think you're our only chance here, Tim. If you can find something, we might be able to help, but otherwise, I don't see how we could do anything." He cleared his throat. "The ghosts are gone."

"We thought the same when Marcel was gone," Jerome intervened, ignoring the last thing Victor said. "Yet we managed to find him. We'll do the same this time. We just have to focus and work our asses off."

Tim was ready to do just that, but he needed a break, since he'd been on his computer for several hours already. The meeting was over, and people started getting to their feet. So did Tim. When Leo moved toward Marcel, Tim pushed him back to York, but he didn't stop to see York's reaction. Instead, he turned to Victor. "Are you heading out already?"

Victor nodded. "I want to contact a few people and ask them if they noticed anything odd happening in the city lately."

"I'll walk you to your car, then."

The smile on Victor's face was enough for Tim to be happy he'd offered. He quickly went to the office he shared with Lindsey to grab his jacket and pack up his computer, and when he came out, it was to find York and Victor talking. Leo was close by, scowling at Victor, and Tim stopped next to him. "I need you to drive York home," he said.

"Why would I do that?"

"Because I'm asking you? I'd normally do it, but I have something to do with Victor." Tim had another idea, and while Victor might say no, Tim hoped he wouldn't. Surely Victor had to eat dinner. Why wouldn't he want to eat it with Tim?

"So you're asking me to do you a favor."

"I'm asking you to find your heart in that big chest of yours and take pity on York. Besides, don't think I didn't see you pawing him."

Leo suddenly looked like he wanted to kill Tim. It was an expression Tim was used to seeing on people's faces when they had to deal with him.

"I was just comforting him. He was terrified," Leo said gruffly.

Tim patted Leo's big arm. "Well, you can continue comforting him. Take him home to the clan. You're going there anyway."

"I could have plans," Leo called out after Tim as Tim walked toward Victor and York.

"You don't," Tim called back without looking at Leo. "The only friends you have are here, and they're all busy."

"Fuck you!"

Tim laughed. He gently patted York's shoulder when he reached him and Victor, and while he was happy to see the two of them talking in a friendly way, he had things to do. "Leo will take you home," he told York.

York's eyes widened. "What? Why?"

"I'm taking Victor to his car, but I was hoping he'd want to grab dinner with me." Tim looked at Victor. "Is that something you'd want to do?"

"I suppose my phone calls can wait," Victor said.

Tim grinned. "Great. I'm buying."

"You don't have to do that."

"Maybe not, but I want to." Tim wanted to do so many things with Victor and *to* him, and he hoped this was the first step to getting all of that. He'd be fine if it wasn't, but something about Victor pulled him in, and he wanted to see what would happen next.

Victor was bemused by Tim's obvious interest, but he couldn't say he disliked it. If anything, he felt the opposite. He wanted Tim to be interested in him, even though it could lead to so many problems it gave him a headache just to think about them.

He had to keep in mind that Tim was nothing like Barton. For one, Tim was much younger and closer to Victor's age than Barton had been. He wasn't as rich as Barton, and from what Victor had seen, he hadn't been raised as a spoiled child who was given everything he wanted.

Barton had. Victor wished he'd seen it sooner, but when he had, he and Barton were already together, and he had been too late. Some days, he wondered if he would have given in and dated Barton at all if Barton hadn't pushed so hard. He'd somehow managed to convince Victor that Victor liked him, and for several reasons, Victor had gone along with it.

But Tim was doing nothing of the sort. He was interested in Victor, and he was pretty open about it, but he always allowed Victor to say no and take a step back. Maybe that was why Victor didn't want to. Maybe Victor's heart was finally thawing after it had been broken so harshly by Barton.

Or maybe it had never been broken at all. Maybe Victor had told himself it was because he'd thought that was how he should feel after breaking up with his boyfriend.

Victor was confused, and spending time with Tim wasn't helping him feel less so. That wasn't going to stop him, though.

"Ready to go?" Tim asked.

Victor realized he'd been staring. He felt his cheeks heat, and he looked away. "Ready when you are."

"Well, I'm ready now, so that's good." Tim turned to the others, who were still lingering in the office, talking in small groups. "Victor and I are leaving. See you tomorrow!"

As if Tim expected someone to ask him to stay back, he grabbed Victor's arm and pulled him along as he walked out of the office. He'd gone into his office to grab his jacket, and he was carrying a messenger bag that no doubt contained his computer.

"So, is there anything you don't eat?" he asked.

"I'm game to try pretty much anything. There are a few things I don't eat, but it's specific ingredients, not a kind of cuisine. Whatever you have in mind, I'm sure it'll be great."

Tim paused next to a big car. He was grinning as if Victor had offered him the moon, and it made Victor wonder why Tim seemed so enthusiastic to spend time with him. Sure, he was clearly interested in more than friendship with Victor, but no one had ever seemed so happy to spend time with Victor.

Maybe he'd been dating the wrong people.

Tim unlocked what was clearly his car and dropped his bag into the trunk. "There's a really nice Mexican restaurant just around the corner. It's family-owned, and it's real Mexican food. Is that something you think you can enjoy?"

"I'm sure I'll love it."

Tim seemed satisfied. He closed the trunk of his car, locked it again, and guided Victor down the street.

"What do you think is happening with the people vanishing?" he asked as they walked.

"Nothing good," Victor said with a sigh. "I don't know as much as I should about magic, but considering what Curt was doing with the shifters he kidnapped, it's easy to imagine what he might be doing with these humans. I'm afraid we're going to start finding bodies soon."

Tim grimaced. "That's what I was afraid of, too. I wish there was more I could do, but I don't know what. It's like these people just vanished. There's no way for me to find them, no matter how much I try. They're not using their credit cards or accounts, and their phones are off. Whoever is taking them knows what they're doing."

"I wish there was more I could do, too, but unfortunately, that's not going to happen until some of these people start dying, and that's not what we're aiming for."

Tim nodded. Victor could see the restaurant Tim had been talking about at the end of the street, so he knew the conversation was almost over. He didn't mind. There was nothing either of them could do for his people, and talking about it wouldn't solve anything.

"Do you still think your ex is involved?" Tim asked.

Victor wished Tim had never brought Barton up, but Victor would need to tell everyone about him anyway if Barton was involved. He wasn't looking forward to it, but he wasn't ashamed of what had happened.

"I think it's a possibility. He's rich, has many contacts, and always gets what he wants."

Tim wrinkled his nose as he pushed open the restaurant door. "That doesn't sound like someone you'd date."

Victor was amused. "Doesn't it? What kind of guy do you think I usually date?"

Tim's grin was cheeky. "Guys like me, maybe?"

Victor laughed. He couldn't believe he'd gone from talking about Barton to laughing in just a few moments, but that was the kind of thing Tim did to him. He made Victor happy in a way Barton never had.

Tim talked to one of the waitresses, and she led the way to one of the tables in the back. The air smelled amazing, and it made Victor's stomach growl. Almost all the tables were occupied, which Victor hoped meant the food here was good.

"I love this place, and I love that it's close to the office," Tim said as he sat down in his chair.

"You sound like you're a regular here."

"That's because I am. I'm spoiled at home with good meals, but this place is great."

"Can I ask about your family? If I remember right, you live with your clan."

Tim leaned forward. "I do. I know that for many humans, it sounds weird, but it's just how we are. Even though we're not all related, we're still family. We're clan." Tim shrugged. "And while some people like Jerome leave the clan, I enjoy it."

"Do you have siblings?" Tim felt like he should have siblings.

"Unfortunately, I don't. I'm sure you're aware of it, but dragons don't have many children. The fact that my aunt and uncle had two kids is an oddity, even with our clan. What about you? Do you have siblings?"

"I do, and I can't imagine my life without my three brothers."

Tim bounced in his chair. "Three brothers? That sounds like a rowdy house."

"Especially since two of them are also psychics. The only one in the family who isn't is my brother, Olsen."

Tim whistled. "That couldn't have been easy for him."

"It wasn't, but our parents never treated him any differently. He learned how to deal with ghosts just like the rest of us, even though he's never had to use what our parents taught us."

Talking with Tim was easy in a way it hadn't been with Barton. Eventually, Victor would have to stop comparing the two, but for now, it was the easiest way to make himself believe that Tim was different from Barton.

Tim didn't try to order food for Victor the way Barton routinely did when they were together. He didn't push Victor into ordering wine with his food instead of a soda. He didn't steer the conversation away from what interested Victor, and he didn't tell Victor how stupid the things he was talking about were.

Tim was nothing like Barton. Victor liked him even more for that.

The dinner flew by, and by the time they were done eating, Victor realized they'd been sitting there for two hours. It wasn't late, but Victor knew that the restaurant owners would want to give their table to other customers, so he got to his feet once they were done eating.

Tim looked startled. "Where are you going?"

Victor gestured at the people standing in line at the restaurant door. "We should probably go."

"I hadn't realized it had gotten so late. I'm sorry I kept you here for so long."

"Don't be. It was the most fun I had in a long time."

"Then you must not have a lot of fun in your life."

"I didn't, until recently."

Tim nodded as if he understood. "That's sad, but you found me and the others now. We'll make your life fun."

Victor had no doubt about that, because they already were.

Tim insisted on paying, which was something Barton had done because he wanted to show off how much money he had. It made Victor bristle until Tim promised that Victor could pay the next time they had dinner together. That made Victor feel better, because it was another sign that Tim was different, but also because it meant they'd have dinner together again.

He took a deep breath once they were back on the sidewalk. He didn't want the evening to end, but it was time. They were silent as they reached Victor's car and just a bit awkward. Victor wasn't sure how to end the evening, but the words died on his lips when he turned toward Tim to say goodbye.

Tim was staring at him in a way he'd never looked at Victor before. Victor swallowed, unsure what to make of it.

"Would it be okay if I kissed you?" Tim asked.

His voice was just a bit rough, and his tone went straight to Victor's cock. He swallowed, then nodded. "You can," he whispered.

He didn't have to say it twice. Tim stepped forward, crowding Victor against the car. He leaned in, and Victor held his breath until their lips touched. Then he threw his arms around Tim's neck, holding on for dear life as Tim kissed him.

Victor wanted to stop comparing Tim to Barton, but he couldn't get over how different this kiss was from the ones he and Barton had exchanged. Tim was forceful, but it felt obvious that he would step back as soon as Victor wanted this to end.

But Victor never wanted it to end. He pushed himself closer, drinking in Tim and the sounds he made as they kissed. He didn't know what he was ready for, if this would be too much or not enough, but he was done resisting.

Now he had to convince his heart and his brain that Tim would be good for him.

CHAPTER FIVE

Victor was still thinking about how Curt was accomplishing what he was doing a few days later. No one he'd contacted was able to come to the city, which was a problem. If Curt was using magic, Victor and the others needed a mage who could recognize and fight it. They'd been taken by surprise with Marcel, because they hadn't known about Curt's girlfriend, but now they did. There was no way she was doing this on her own, which meant they'd need help to defeat her and Curt.

Victor tapped his fingertips on the table. He was in his motel room on the phone, trying to find a mage who could help them. It was hard to find real ones, though. Just like psychics, some mages faked their power and used it to rob people. Victor wouldn't have been surprised if this was the kind of person Barton was doing business with, but Curt needed real mages to make things work.

He quickly dialed Tim's number. They hadn't seen each other since they'd had dinner together and kissed by Victor's car, but they'd been texting and calling. Victor felt slightly awkward. He'd never thought he'd go through this dating thing again, and he wasn't sure how to behave. When he met Barton, Barton had swept him off his feet, and he'd barely had to do anything. He didn't want his relationship with Tim to go that way, but he felt like an idiot most of the time. Tim hadn't said anything about it, but he wasn't the kind of guy who would.

"Victor!" Tim said as he answered.

The sound of his voice made Victor smile. "I hope I'm not bothering you?"

"You could never bother me. Do you need anything? Are you coming to the office?"

"That might be the easiest way to do this."

"Do what?"

"I've been poking around trying to find real mages, but it isn't easy. My parents were able to give me a list of names, and my brothers added several to that list, but there's no way for me to know which of these mages are real. I've looked through social media, and it helps, but it's still a lot of work for not many results."

"So you want me to look through these people's lives and find out whether or not they have magic powers?"

"Pretty much. Is that something you think you can help me with?"

"Come to the office. We'll look through things together, and hopefully, we'll find a mage who can help us."

Victor wasn't sure he'd trust a mage he'd found this way, but they might not have another option. None of them knew mages, and even if they contacted the people on his list, there was no way to know if they were real mages, if they were willing to help them, if they would try to take advantage of them, or worse, if they were working with Curt and Barton.

Victor still had no proof that Barton was working with Curt, but since Curt needed mages to do whatever he was doing, it meant he needed money to pay those mages. Victor didn't know much about Curt, but this was exactly the kind of situation Barton would insert himself in.

Barton was still calling Victor. Victor hadn't answered, and he wasn't listening to the voice messages. He also wasn't reading any of the texts, although that was harder. He wanted to find out what Barton wanted, yet at the same time, he wasn't willing to let the man into his life again. It wouldn't be good, and Victor wanted to focus on the future rather than the past.

He was glad to leave the motel room. He really needed to find an apartment, since it seemed he was going to stick around for a while, but none of the ones he'd seen had been the right fit. He was getting desperate, but he'd started working again, so money wouldn't be a problem.

He was a bit hesitant when he reached the office. He was getting used to being here, so he walked through the waiting area and headed directly to the office Tim and Lindsey shared. It was tiny, but that was where Tim worked, so it was where Victor had to go.

Sure enough, when he poked his head through the open door, he found Tim at his desk, his focus on his computer, his fingers flying on the keyboard. Victor took a moment to look at him. Then he cleared his throat.

Tim's smile was delighted when he looked up and saw Victor.

"That was fast. Come in, come in. I grabbed a chair so you wouldn't have to stand behind me." He patted the empty chair next to him. "This way, you can see the screen with me."

Victor wasn't sure how to behave, but since Tim was acting as if nothing had happened between them, he did the same.

That only lasted until he sat down. Tim twisted in his chair, quickly kissed Victor's cheek, and then turned back to his computer. It left Victor blinking, but Tim was already talking about his work, not giving Victor the time to obsess over what had just happened.

"So, I was wondering how hard it would be to find a real mage, and I started poking around. You weren't kidding when you said you didn't know if you could trust these people. Do you know how many reviews and complaints there are of fake mages who took people's money and vanished?"

"I'm not surprised." Victor took out his phone and pulled

up his father's text message. "Here. These are names I got from my family. I've already been through the first few, and I don't think any of them can help us. Hopefully, some of the others can."

Tim cracked his knuckles. "If there's a real mage in town, I'll find them."

Victor had no doubt Tim would. The problem was that Victor didn't know whether or not there was a real mage in the city. With so many people living in the same area, there probably was, but most good psychics didn't advertise on the Internet, and Victor suspected the same went for mages. It wouldn't be easy to find someone who could work with them, but they didn't have a choice.

An hour later, they didn't have anything to show for their research. Tim was getting impatient, even though he was used to looking for needles in haystacks. This was getting them nowhere, but finding a mage was urgent. They needed someone who could tell them what Curt was doing and possibly make sure Curt failed.

Tim huffed and leaned back in his chair. His eyes burned, and while rubbing them gave him a little relief, it wouldn't last.

"This is getting us nowhere," Victor murmured.

Tim wanted to kiss him, but he was trying to be professional. "Maybe we should try another approach."

"What approach?"

Victor looked tired. The dark smudges under his eyes were getting darker, which made Tim wonder if he was sleeping. If he wasn't, what was the problem? Was he just worried about Curt and what the shifter was doing, or was there more? Maybe something to do with his ex-boyfriend?

Tim wanted to ask, but he wasn't sure it was his place yet.

He and Victor weren't together, or at least, they hadn't talked about being together. Maybe it was time to do so, but Tim couldn't help but feel that wasn't as important as stopping Curt. Surely Victor felt the same way.

Or maybe this was the perfect moment to do something like that. Maybe they needed something good out of this mess.

"It would be good if we could talk to someone who worked with a mage," Victor said.

He was tapping his fingertips on the desk, something he often did when he was thinking. Tim found it endearing, but he didn't dare say anything about it.

Victor's words finally penetrated. Tim straightened, wondering how he could have been so stupid. "You say we need someone who already worked with a mage," he said slowly.

Victor frowned as he nodded. "Yes. Wouldn't it make sense?"

"It would, and I should have thought about this sooner." Tim reached for his phone on the desk. He quickly dialed a number he knew from memory, raising a finger when Victor opened his mouth, no doubt to ask him what he was doing.

He listened for a moment, praying Elijah would answer, grinning in relief when his alpha did. "Elijah?" he asked.

"Did you expect someone else, considering you called my number? Is everything okay?"

Tim raised a thumb at Victor. "Actually, Victor and I have a bit of a problem."

"What kind of problem?"

"We're trying to locate a mage. We're having a bit of trouble because we can't tell whether or not the people we're finding are real mages or if they're just acting like they are to earn money. We also need someone we can trust, which is even harder to identify. You wouldn't happen to know a mage, would you?"

"Yes, I do know a few mages. Does this have anything to do with the vanishing humans?"

"Yeah. We think that whoever's taking them is using magic on them, which is why we need a mage."

"Well, if you're looking into that, you need to turn on the TV."

The words made Tim frown. "Why? What's happening?"

"Just put on the news, Tim. I'll contact the mages I know and ask if they can help. I wouldn't hold my breath if I were you. Considering the press conference, I don't think many of them will want to."

"Press conference?"

"I'm watching it, too."

Tim quickly hung up and turned his attention to his computer. He already had a browser open, so it didn't take long to type in the address of a local news station and find what Elijah had been referring to. Tim recognized the mayor, standing behind a podium with microphones in front of him. Several people were hovering behind him, including the chief of police, who was wearing his uniform.

Victor softly swore as Tim turned on the volume.

"The police force is looking into it, and the chief of police and his men are doing everything they can to find the people who've disappeared," the mayor was saying. "Of course, we can't talk about an active investigation. It could put the people who were taken in danger, as well as our police force. We all know many people out there who are dangerous and who could be involved, and some of them aren't human."

"Are you saying shifters are involved?" a woman asked.

"We don't know who's involved as of now. We'll be able to tell you more after the investigation, but we're open to every possibility for now. Shifters have been known to create trouble, so I suggest that most humans stay away from them, at least for now. We have no way to know whether or not they're involved."

Tim gaped at the screen. Had the mayor really just said that shifters were responsible for the humans vanishing?

Tim supposed that, in a way, he was right. Curt was a shifter, and he was the one kidnapping these humans. He was the only one doing so, though. Other shifters had nothing to do with it, and what the mayor was saying would create trouble. Hell, that was probably why he was saying it.

"I should have seen this coming," Victor murmured.

Tim blindly reached for Victor's hand. He squeezed it when he found it, but he didn't look away from the screen.

"What do you think the shifters are doing with the humans they're taking?" a man asked the mayor. He was taking notes on his phone as he spoke.

"Again, I never said shifters were involved."

"But you sure implied it," Tim muttered.

The mayor continued talking, but Tim wasn't listening. Nothing the guy was saying made sense or was important, not after he'd implied shifters were involved. His words would make an already uneasy relationship between humans and shifters even worse, and that was the last thing everyone needed. What had he been thinking?

When Tim turned to look at Victor, he realized how pale the man was. He didn't understand why, but he leaned closer, needing to make sure Victor was okay. "Are you all right? Is it because of the press conference?"

Victor bit his lower lip. He was still staring at the screen, but Tim realized he wasn't looking at the mayor but rather at the chief of police. Tim couldn't remember the guy's name, but the bottom of his stomach dropped.

"Your ex isn't the chief of police, is he?" he asked.

Victor's eyes widened. "No. But I know him. He's my ex's brother, and the mayor is my ex's childhood friend."

That didn't make Tim feel better. "Is this one of the reasons you think your ex is involved?"

Victor sighed and leaned back in his chair. He looked even more tired, and Tim wanted nothing more than to wrap him into his arms and shield him from whatever was happening.

"Let's just say that this press conference doesn't surprise me, just like the fact that the mayor and the chief of police are getting involved doesn't. If Barton has anything to do with this, it makes sense for him to involve these two guys. They'll ensure he won't be hurt by whatever's going on and that, in the end, all three of them will gain from it. Barton *has* to be involved. I don't have proof, but I know it."

Tim nodded and wrapped an arm around Victor's shoulders. When Victor relaxed and leaned against him, Tim knew he'd done the right thing. He kissed the top of Victor's head, something he wouldn't normally be able to do, since Victor was a bit taller than him. In their chairs, though, it was easy.

"I can't promise you everything will be okay, but we'll do everything we can to make sure Barton and his friends can't hurt anyone."

"We might already be too late. What if they hurt the people they're taking? What are they doing to them?" Victor's tone was growing panicky. "We need to do more, but I don't know what. Maybe I should talk to Barton."

Tim shook his head. "That's the last thing you need to do. He'll use you, and I don't want anything to happen to you."

"I wouldn't let him do anything."

Tim arched a brow and looked down at Victor. "What if he said he'd let these people go if you went back to him? Wouldn't you say yes?"

Victor sighed heavily. "I would," he confirmed.

"Because you're a good person. Barton isn't, and we're going to have to deal with him, but no one is going out there on their own. I don't want to lose you, and I know I'm not the only one."

"I just feel powerless, you know? I knew Barton was involved, and I knew it had to mean that the mayor and the chief of police were, too. I should have told you guys about it."

"Maybe, but even if we'd known, we wouldn't have been able to do anything. This press conference doesn't change anything."

"I'm pretty sure it changed everything. You heard the mayor. He said he believes shifters are involved, which means half the city at least will take his words as an opportunity to harass the shifters who live here. This isn't going to end well, Tim."

Tim agreed, but what could they do?

CHAPTER SIX

Victor stared at his phone as if it might bite him. That was how he felt, especially since he'd decided to call Barton.

He still wasn't sure it was a good idea, but he had to try. Barton *had* to be involved, and Victor hoped to be able to change his ex's mind. He was ready to try anything to save the people who'd been taken, but he doubted it would work. Barton didn't do anything that didn't benefit him in some way, and this wouldn't. Victor wouldn't be surprised if, like Tim had suggested, Barton used this to try to get Victor back.

What would Victor do if that was the case? Could he say no when he'd be able to save so many people? Could he say yes when it meant giving up his new friends, Tim, and the life he'd been building away from Barton?

Barton had never been physically abusive. He thought violence was beneath him and that he was too sophisticated to use it, especially against someone he was supposed to love. No, his kind of abuse was sneakier. Victor hadn't realized that it was abuse until after he left, but now, he knew.

He didn't want to think about what had happened, how Barton had convinced him they should be together, and how he'd kept Victor by his side for so long. Victor had known that what Barton was doing was wrong, but he'd been terrified of losing him. He'd been an idiot, and he couldn't afford to be an idiot a second time.

Victor snatched the phone from the table. His hand trembled, but he didn't let that stop him. Even if Barton somehow managed to find him, he wasn't planning on staying here at the motel for much longer. He'd already packed his bags, and he was ready to sleep in his car if it meant being safe from Barton. He'd booked a motel room closer to the office, though, at least for a few days. He'd decide what to do later.

He unlocked the phone and opened his missed calls. He'd saved Barton's number again, mostly because he wanted to know it was Barton calling him, but the sight of the name on his screen made his stomach churn. He took a deep breath, then another, praying he wouldn't throw up while he was talking to Barton.

Then, he pressed Barton's name with his thumb and started the call.

It took Barton several rings to pick up. "I didn't think I'd hear from you," he said when he did.

He already knew it was Victor. He'd somehow gotten his hands on Victor's new number, and he'd assumed Victor would be happy to hear from him. Even though Victor had dumped him and ran away from him, Barton only saw what he wanted to see.

Victor wanted to say something, but the words felt stuck in his throat. He took a deep breath, trying to force his shoulders to relax. "I wouldn't be calling if I didn't feel it was necessary," he said, trying to keep his tone as harsh as he could.

Barton didn't seem to notice. "I have to say I'm pleased that you finally called. Are you coming home?"

The thought made Victor shudder in horror. "If I were going home, I'd be going to my parents."

"Are you still angry? You know, I don't understand what I did. We were perfectly fine and happy one moment, and the next, you'd vanished. I feel you owe me at least an explanation."

"Is that why you've been calling me? Because you want an explanation?"

"I was worried about you. I love you."

Victor resisted the urge to snap that Barton only loved himself. "Well, I don't love you. I'm not coming back, so you can stop calling me."

Barton barely missed a beat. "Yet, you're calling *me*."

"Because I want to know what you're up to."

"What do you mean?"

"I saw the press conference. If your brother and your best friend are involved, it means you are, too. What are the three of you up to?" Victor didn't mention that he thought Barton was working with Curt. He didn't want to mention Curt at all because he didn't want Barton to realize that he knew.

"Would I really go around kidnapping humans?"

Victor snorted. "Yes, you would if it could benefit you. So I'm asking why you're doing it. What are you trying to obtain from this?"

"I'd tell you, but first, I'd need you to be on our side. Is that why you're calling? Because you're coming back to me?"

Victor wanted to scream and ask if Barton had been listening to him, but he didn't dare. "I'm not coming back. I want to know what you're doing."

"It's a pity I can't tell you, then. You really should think about it. If you come back, you not only would be with me again, but you'd also have more money and power than you can ever dream of having on your own. Let me take care of you, Victor. I love you, and I know you still love me. You wouldn't be calling me if you didn't."

How had Victor ever found Barton attractive and suave? He'd been seduced, and it didn't make sense, although he supposed hindsight was twenty-twenty. At the time, he hadn't seen Barton for what he was. Now, he could, and the thought of going back to him made his skin crawl.

"I don't love you, and I wouldn't come back to you even if you were the last man on earth," Victor snapped. He was losing his patience, but he doubted Barton would tell him anything he didn't already know. The man might be an ass-hole, but he wasn't stupid.

Now Victor knew for sure that Barton was involved. It made him feel better, but it still didn't tell him what he was supposed to do with the knowledge. He supposed he and the others could keep an eye on Barton and his two accomplices, but would that be enough?

"You're taking innocent people," he said. Against all odds, he still had hope he could change Barton's mind. "I don't know what you're doing to them, but it can't be good. You're hurting them, aren't you?"

Barton tsked. "They're not like us, Victor. They're not mages or psychics. They're just human."

"So? It doesn't mean they're useless and that we can hurt them."

"They're meaningless. If using them means I get what I want, then I will. You can be with me or against me, and I know you'd rather be with me."

Barton still didn't get it, did he? "I'm never coming back to you," Victor whispered. "Stop calling me. Stop trying to find me. You're heartless, and I could never be with someone like you, someone so cruel that you think humans are meaning-less, someone who takes people who've never done anything and hurts them, or worse, kills them. I don't know what you're doing, Barton, but I know it's not good, and I want nothing to do with it."

Victor hung up without allowing Barton to add anything. He threw his phone onto the table, glaring at it as he panted. He felt like he'd run a marathon, but he'd only talked to Barton.

He knew Barton was definitely involved now, and so were the chief of police and the mayor. They didn't care that they were hurting people. Hell, it was probably fun to them. They had no respect for life or anything beyond themselves, and that wasn't going to change.

But what was Victor supposed to do with this information? On his own, the answer was nothing. With his friends, maybe he'd be able to save at least a few lives.

He was going to try, at the very least. Barton wasn't his responsibility, but Victor still felt the need to step in and try to fix what Barton was breaking.

He had no idea whether or not he'd be able to.

Tim wasn't sure why Victor had called for a meeting, but it couldn't be good. After the press conference, Victor had distanced himself, and Tim hadn't pushed. He understood that Victor's ex was a sore spot, and while he was dying to know what had happened between them, he didn't dare ask for more details. Whatever Victor's ex had done to Victor, it still hurt Victor, and Tim didn't want to make it worse. If he and Victor were meant to be together, they would be. Tim had all the time in the world, and he wanted Victor to feel comfortable with him. That would only happen if he allowed Victor to do this at his own pace and in his own time.

He looked around the break room. Everyone was there, including York and Leo. York had driven in with Tim that morning, eager to help at the office. He still steered clear of Marcel and Jerome when he saw them, but he didn't seem to have a problem with Tim and Lindsey. He didn't talk much to Will, but the fact that Will was human probably helped York feel more comfortable around him than he was around Jerome and Marcel.

Tim had been surprised when he'd found York working. He'd taken him to the office several times because he thought York could use a change of scenery, and instead of finding him in the break room where he'd left him, he'd been in the waiting area, talking to a woman. He'd been reassuring her, and when Will had come into the waiting area, York had guided her toward his office. Since then, he'd become an unofficial secretary, and he seemed to like the work.

"Not that I don't enjoy seeing all of you," Marcel said, "But why are we here?"

Victor cleared his throat. He was pacing the small space between the back of the chairs around the table and the wall. "I'm sure everyone saw the press conference," he started.

"I wanted to strangle the mayor," Lindsey said with a growl. "I can't believe he threw shifters under the bus that way."

Victor's chuckle was humorless. "I can. I know him and the chief of police." Victor stopped pacing and raked a hand through his hair, messing it up.

Tim's fingers itched to stroke the hair back into place, but he stayed where he was.

"And by that, I mean I know them personally. I dated the chief of police's brother, and he happens to be the mayor's best friend."

There was a moment of silence as everyone in the room digested what Victor had said. Then, the questions started. "What does any of that mean?" Jerome demanded to know.

Victor raised his hands. "I'll explain. I don't particularly enjoy talking about Barton, but I see that I need to." He licked his lips. He was carefully avoiding looking at anyone, which made Tim's heart hurt a bit.

Whatever had happened with his ex-boyfriend, Victor didn't want to talk about it, and Tim could understand that. He'd had bad relationships before, but somehow, he suspected none of them had been as bad as the relationship between Victor and Barton.

"When I met Barton, I was an untrained psychic. My parents taught my brothers and me everything they knew, but Barton was older and successful. He told me I could have anything I wanted if I trained with him, and I was stupid enough to believe him. So I moved in with him, and I started working for him." Victor sucked in a breath. "Our relationship changed soon after that. We became involved."

"Wait," Lindsey said. "How old is Barton? Because you said he's the chief of police's brother."

"He is, and like I just mentioned, he's older than me. Seventeen years older than me, if you want to be more precise."

"And how old were you when you met him?"

Victor looked away. "In my early twenties. He was my first relationship, but that doesn't excuse the fact that I stayed with him for so long. Anyway, I eventually left him because I didn't like how he treated his clients. He made them pay handsomely, and he didn't hesitate to make up things even when he couldn't contact the people he was paid to contact. He comes from a wealthy family, but he never has enough money."

"Why are you telling us this?" Jerome asked.

"Because I suspected he was involved with Curt, and now, I'm sure he is, especially after the press conference. If his brother and his best friend are in this, that means he is, too. I called him, and he confirmed it."

"You called him?" Tim asked as he got to his feet.

"I didn't want to, but I needed to know. He didn't say they were working with Curt, but he admitted he and his accomplices are responsible for the disappearances. I doubt they're taking these people from the streets themselves, which means they're working with someone, and who else could it be? Why would they be kidnapping humans if not to use them with Curt?"

Tim sat back down. Victor didn't need him to fuss over him, especially not in front of everyone else. Tim would make sure Victor was okay later, once they were alone, but for now, he had to focus on what Victor was saying, not on how painful it obviously was for him to rehash all of it.

"How does this help us?" Leo asked.

Tim cleared his throat. "Now that I know at least three people involved with Curt, I can start digging into their lives, and as long as Jerome is okay with it, I can hack their computers, phones, and anything else I can get my hands on."

"Do it," Jerome said with a grunt.

"It's illegal," Tim pointed out.

"It's also illegal for them to kidnap people and possibly kill them. We need to know what's going on, and if this is the only way, I won't stop you."

Tim nodded. He'd do it even if it meant that in the end, Jerome fired him, but he didn't think it would happen. He still didn't have the best relationship with his cousin, but they'd been working together for several weeks now, and he thought Jerome had come to begrudgingly respect him. He hoped he'd be able to find out more about whatever Barton and the others were planning to save the people they'd taken and show Jerome that hiring him had been the best idea he'd ever had.

Even though Jerome hadn't been the one who had it.

"So we're assuming these four guys are behind the disappearances," Marcel said slowly. "Why are they doing it?"

"Well, Barton and his accomplices are probably doing it for power and the money," Victor said. "It's all they're interested in. I know Curt thinks shifters should be in charge of humanity and that they're better than us lowly humans, but Barton doesn't care about that, even though he does believe that plain humans are under him. He parrots the words if it means he gets what he wants, but he's not an ideologist or anything like that. He's just interested in himself and what he can gain from all of this."

"Does this change anything?" Leo asked. "I mean, what do we think Curt and these guys are doing with the humans they kidnap? Does knowing about the people involved help us find that out?"

"I'm guessing Curt is the one who needs the humans," Victor said as he dropped into his chair and leaned forward. "Since he used shifters in the past to raise an army of ghosts, I'm guessing he's attempting to do something similar. Maybe he thought people wouldn't care about humans, and they're easier to control and find. There are plenty of humans in the city, but not so many shifters."

"And what's the mayor doing for Curt?" Lindsey asked.

Tim sucked in a breath. "He's making shifters a target. Many people will use what he said during the press conference as an excuse to attack shifters, or at the very least, to keep an eye on them. It means they'll be distracted and that maybe the mayor and Curt can use humans to attack shifters even if Curt's ghostly army isn't enough."

Curt wanted an army of ghosts because he'd be able to control them, and because there were plenty of ghosts around, but he might not even need it anymore.

Victor looked around the room. These people would all help him stop Barton and Curt, but would they be enough? With the mayor and the chief of police involved, they might need more people, but asking for help would mean putting those people in danger, and Victor wasn't sure he could deal with that.

"We need more people," Jerome declared.

Even though it was what Victor had been thinking, his stomach still churned. "I could try dealing with Barton on my own," he said.

Jerome shook his head. "It's too dangerous."

"I can still do it."

"I don't want to lose anyone if we can avoid it at all. Besides, considering it's now open season on shifters, I think every single shifter in the city has a reason to be involved." He looked at Tim. "Do you think Elijah and the clan would want to be involved?"

Tim leaned back in his chair. "I've already called Elijah. Victor and I needed help finding a mage, and he said he'd look into it. He's the one who told me about the press conference, actually. He sounded pissed, and while I haven't seen him in a while, I know he'll do anything he can to protect the clan. If it means fighting beside us, he'll do it."

Victor's stomach churned. He had people he could involve, too. His brothers wouldn't hesitate to step into the fight if it meant protecting him, but could he ask that of them?

On the one hand, they were adults, and both Roslin and Donahue worked as psychics. They had experience, and they would be useful, since Victor was the only experienced psychic here. On the other hand, they were Victor's brothers, and he was terrified something would happen to them if they got involved. He knew he should give them the opportunity to decide for themselves, but he'd never forgive himself if something happened to them.

His family had never liked Barton, and it had been hard to deal with that. Victor had reacted by putting more distance between himself and his family, and Barton had encouraged him. Now, Victor knew that abusers isolated their victims, and that was what Barton had been doing. Victor should have listened to his family when they said there was something off about Barton and that he wasn't the right kind of guy for Victor, but Victor had been young, and he'd thought he knew everything. By the time he'd realized his family was right, it had been too late for him to get out of Barton's grasp.

But he *was* out now. He was free from Barton, and he was actively fighting against him. His brothers would jump on the opportunity to do the same, and Victor couldn't take that away from them. Besides, they'd kick his ass if he didn't tell them what was happening.

He took his phone out, only vaguely listening to what the others were saying. He pulled up the group text he shared with his brothers, trying to find a way to write all of this down. In the end, it wasn't that complicated.

Barton is involved in something bad. He and his accomplices are kidnapping people, and I'm working with people trying to stop them. We need help, though.

He could already see that Olsen was answering. If there was one brother in particular that Victor wanted to protect, it was Olsen, but Olsen had never let his lack of psychic power keep him from a fight. If Victor and the others were going to fight, so would Olsen.

I'm in, Olsen answered.

Both Roslin and Donahue were also writing. Victor stared at the three dots dancing on the screen, then, one after the other, his brothers' words appeared.

I'm always ready to kick ass, especially Barton's. When do you need us? And where?

That was from Donahue. Victor would never forget when Donahue had punched Barton in the face. He'd been horrified then, and he'd taken Barton's side, but now, he understood why Donahue had done it. Violence was never a good answer, but Barton had it coming. Hell, Victor kind of wished he'd been the one to punch Barton in the face.

I can leave now if you need me. I'll pick up Olsen and Donahue, or we can come in three cars. What do you think, Vic? Roslin didn't even ask what Victor needed from them. None of them had.

Victor's heart swelled in his chest. His brothers were ready to do anything for him because they loved him. This was love, not what Barton had felt for him. Barton wanted to own Victor, and it had nothing to do with love.

I'm sending you an address, he typed. *I'm already here, staying at a motel. The sooner you can get here, the better it will be.*

Are you planning on telling Mom and Dad? Olsen asked.

Victor cringed. *Maybe once all of this is over? I don't want them to get involved.*

They're already going to be pissed that you're in the city and you haven't told anyone, Donahue quickly wrote. *I'm pissed, too, but I'll yell at you once you're in front of me.*

I think it would be better for all of us to stay at the same motel, Roslin wrote. *And yes, Victor, we'll all kick your ass once we reach you. How could you keep the fact that you were home a secret from us?*

Great. Now, they were making Victor feel guilty. *I didn't mean to keep it a secret. I was just overwhelmed and busy.*

Yeah, I watched the press conference, Donahue answered. *That's what you're involved in, isn't it?*

Unfortunately, it is, Victor told his brothers. He texted the address of the office. *This is where we all meet. Let me know when the three of you can be here, and I'll make sure everyone else is.*

Give me a day, Roslin texted. *I have something to take care of, but we'll be with you soon. Stay safe in the meantime.*

I'll do my best, Victor answered. *Please, the three of you need to do the same.*

Always, Donahue texted.

Olsen had been mostly silent, but he sent a thumbs-up emoji, telling Victor he'd be there. Victor was both relieved and worried as he put down his phone.

"That was an intense bout of texting," Tim said from beside him.

Victor gave him a tired smile. "Jerome is right. We need more people, and if you're pulling in dragons, I need to do the same with my brothers. They're experienced psychics, and they'll be able to do more than York, Will, and Lindsey."

"Is your non-psychic brother coming, too?"

"I wouldn't be able to keep him away even if I tried. I'm worried about them, but I couldn't keep them away from all this. They live in the city, too, and I'm sure they have friends they want to protect. I need to give them a chance to do so, no matter how terrified I am."

"So we're waiting on more people to arrive," Jerome declared. "Since there's nothing else we can do today, I think the meeting is over. Everyone, let me know when the people we're expecting arrive. We'll have another meeting." Jerome looked around. "Although maybe we should have it somewhere else. I'm not sure more people can fit into this room."

"Maybe you need a bigger office," Tim teased him.

It was good to see Tim and Jerome playing around. Things were still tense between them, but Victor was convinced that eventually, they'd solve their problems.

Family was everything. They needed to stick together, be able to rely on each other, and work together. The situation was complicated enough without adding a family fight to it, so Victor was relieved the two were working things out.

People started getting to their feet and streaming out of the room. Victor closed his eyes and leaned back in his chair, needing a moment to himself.

"How are you feeling?" Tim asked softly.

Victor blinked his eyes open. Tim was leaning toward him, looking worried. Victor forced himself to smile because he didn't want him to worry.

"I'm tired, and I can tell it's going to be a while before I get a good night's sleep, but I'll be fine."

"I don't want you to get hurt." Tim hesitated. "I really like you, Victor. And I'm not saying that I like you as a friend, although that's certainly part of it. I want to kiss you again and do so much more with you."

The smile on Victor's face turned real. "I really like you, too." Maybe this wasn't the right moment for them to do this, or maybe it was. That wasn't the problem. "But I have to admit I'm a bit hesitant after what happened with Barton. I know you're nothing like him, but my heart is battered."

For some reason, that didn't make Tim turn around and

run away. "I can wait for your heart to heal, and maybe I can even help it get better."

Victor stared at him for a moment. "You understand I can't make promises, especially considering everything else?"

Tim took Victor's hand and kissed the back of it. "I don't need promises. I just need you to tell me you'll try."

Victor could do that. "I will. I want to be happy." And he suspected Tim could help with that.

Chapter Seven

Victor looked around with wide eyes. When Tim had said they'd have this meeting in the house where his clan lived, he hadn't said it was a mansion. Hell, it looked more like a palace. There definitely would be more than enough space for all of them to meet. There was more than enough space for Victor's motel room to fit in the entrance of this place.

Tim rubbed the back of his head as he gestured for Victor to follow him. "I know it's a lot," he said.

"It is. This is where you live?"

"Yeah. The clan is like a big family. We all have our personal rooms, but we tend to spend a lot of time together in the communal areas, like the kitchen and the living room."

"How many dragons live here?"

"You'd have to ask Elijah. I could start counting, but it would take me a while."

"That's fine." Victor didn't need a number, anyway.

Tim guided him and his brothers through the house. Victor could hear Olsen and Donahue whispering to each other, and he was tempted to glare at them, but he understood where they were coming from. They hadn't known to expect this any more than Victor.

"So we'll be working with the dragons?" Donahue asked.

Tim smiled at him. "Some of them. Not everyone can be involved. I mean, my grandmother wanted to go out there and kick ass, but our alpha talked her down."

Victor found himself snorting. "I'm sure it wasn't easy."

"It wasn't, but Elijah is used to dealing with us. Have you seen my grandfather again?"

Victor nodded. "He's often hanging around you. He didn't like how those ghosts behaved when they surrounded us in the office, though, and he's been bitching about keeping you safe from them and any other ghosts looking your way. I think he's been moving between you and other members of your family."

"Probably my grandmother. I haven't told her about him yet because I have no idea how she'd react, but I'll have to do that soon."

"I can be there to help, if you want."

Tim took Victor's hand. "That would be great. She'll love you."

Victor didn't miss the way Olsen elbowed Donahue in the ribs and nodded at him and Tim. He glared at them, but they didn't care. Olsen wiggled his eyebrows while Donahue mouthed, "Meeting the family already?"

Victor discreetly flipped them the bird with his free hand. Donahue barked out a laugh, making Tim look at him.

"This is a great place," Donahue said, looking around.

"It really is. We know how lucky we are, although considering how long we live, we need our clan home to be safe and massive."

Victor liked that his brothers were getting along with Tim, but he couldn't help but wonder about the others. Tim had said that the mage who had agreed to work with them had already arrived, and Victor was curious to meet him. They were going to need his help and the help of everyone who was able to do something.

They walked for what felt like half an hour — that was how big the mansion was. Eventually, though, Tim stopped in front of an open door. He pulled Victor through it, and the sound of voices rose. Victor understood why when he saw how many people were gathered there.

He recognized everyone but two men sitting at the table, their heads close together as they quietly spoke. One had to be the mage, but Victor wasn't sure who the other was.

Tim noticed him looking and tilted his chin toward the two men. "The one with the brown hair is Elijah, our alpha. He's talking with Gunter, the mage."

Victor nodded. They had everyone they needed now, and he prayed they would be enough. He wasn't sure what he'd do if otherwise. They couldn't fail, no matter how hard the fight waiting for them would be.

Tim led Victor to the table, and as if it were a signal, everyone started sitting down. Victor ended up next to Gunter, who arched a brow at him.

"I'm Victor," Victor said.

"Gunter. You're one of the psychics, right?"

"I am. You're the mage?"

"Yep. Elijah didn't tell me much of what was happening, just that it's dangerous."

"Yet you're still here?"

Gunter shrugged. "I'm getting paid handsomely."

Victor blinked. They hadn't thought about that part. "You are?" Who was paying him? Victor felt he should contribute, but he wasn't sure he could.

"Don't worry about it," Elijah said, leaning around Gunter. "I'm taking care of it." His voice was deep and grumbly, exactly the kind of voice Victor imagined a dragon would have.

"It's not right for you to pay everything," Victor said.

Elijah waved a hand. "I can afford to pay Gunter once, or even a dozen times. Besides, after the press conference, I want this to be over as much as you do. The mayor put a target on our backs, and I won't stand for that, especially when he's the one actually involved in the kidnappings."

Jerome cleared his throat, getting everyone's attention.

Lindsey pushed his shoulder, and Jerome rolled his eyes before getting to his feet.

"Since there are several new people here today, I thought it would be good to introduce everyone. This is Elijah," he said, pointing at Elijah, who waved around the table. "He's the alpha of this dragon clan, and he offered for us to meet here, considering how many people are involved by now. Next to him is Gunter, a mage." Jerome pointed at Victor's brothers. "And you have to be Victor's brothers."

Donahue wiggled his fingers at Jerome. "I'm Donahue, and these are Olsen and Roslin."

Jerome nodded. "Good. Now that everyone knows who everyone is, we can get to the point." He quickly explained what had happened to Marcel. York was present, too, and he seemed to be trying to disappear into the chair he was sitting on. Leo was next to him, and he quietly said something Victor couldn't hear. It seemed to reassure York, which was all that mattered.

"So, we now know that Curt is probably working with Barton, the mayor, and the chief of police," Jerome finished.

"What are they gaining from this?" Elijah asked. "Because I can understand where Curt's coming from, in a way. Shifters have been treated like pariahs for hundreds of years, and some of us are angry. I'm not saying that what he's doing is right, but I understand what he's getting from it, or rather, what he hopes to get from it. But what about the three humans?"

"Barton is a psychic," Victor said. "I suspect that's why Curt is using him. He wants more ghosts, and the only way to communicate with them is through psychics. As for the mayor and the chief of police, I can only assume they want the same thing Barton wants. More power, more money, and for people to look at them with fear."

"So they don't share Curt's feelings about enslaving

humans and reigning over the country?"

"Not that I know of. Barton believes he's better than every-one, but he's fine with earning money and feeling that way. He doesn't want to reign over people or make decisions. No, Curt is the dangerous one here, and we'll have to be careful. He's using Barton, the mayor, and the chief of police, but he might turn on them if he doesn't get what he wants."

"And what he wants is absolute power."

And the people who wanted that usually never stopped in front of anything. Curt had been using and killing shifters, and now, he'd moved on to humans. He wouldn't stop until he got what he wanted, no matter how many lives he had to sacrifice.

That was what made him dangerous.

Tim wasn't surprised by what Victor was saying about Barton, but he wished things were different. He didn't want Victor to feel guilty or awkward, or like any of this was his fault, and it was clear that part of him believed that.

"This is all nice and good," Gunter interrupted. "But what am *I* doing here?"

"Weren't you listening when I explained what these people did to my brother?" Jerome snapped.

Tim cleared his throat. They didn't need Jerome bickering with anyone, least of all the only mage who'd agreed to work with them. Once he had Gunter's attention, he smiled at him. "We don't think they're using shifters anymore, but rather, that they've moved on to humans."

Gunter frowned. "Are you talking about the humans who've been vanishing?"

Tim suspected Gunter lived in the city. The vanishing people had gotten a lot of attention these past few days, but not outside of where they lived. He probably wouldn't have known about them if he weren't from here.

Tim nodded. "Yes. It's the only thing that makes sense."

"I don't know that it does. I understand taking shifters and using their life energy, but humans? They don't have nearly as much life energy as most shifters. There are a few exceptions, but it would take a large number of humans to do what you could do with one shifter."

"Which is why they've taken so many humans in the past month. We're at fifteen, and I have no doubt that number will grow."

Gunter was still frowning, but he was clearly thinking about what Tim had said. "So that's why you asked me to help. You think these guys are using magic to take life energy from humans. Have bodies been found yet?"

The fact that Gunter's mind had gone there meant they probably would start to find them soon. Gunter wasn't the only one who'd mentioned that these humans were going to die eventually, but Tim had hoped they'd find them alive.

For the most recent disappearances, they might be able to, but he doubted they could for the oldest ones. They didn't even know when the first people had been taken. It had to have been after they'd found Marcel, but there was no way to know exactly when. He'd found many reports of people disappearing, but there was no way for him to be sure that Barton and his accomplices had taken all these people.

"We're not sure," Victor intervened. He turned slightly in his seat to look at Gunter. "Bodies are found every day. We're not quite sure what to look for in them, so we don't know if they died because of something Barton and his people did or from other causes."

"I see. Have the bodies of some of the people who've disappeared popped up, then?"

"Not that we know of."

"They're going to, eventually. If Curt and Barton are using

these people as magical batteries, they'll drain them soon."

"I'll keep an eye on the news," Tim said.

"Holy fuck," someone at the table breathed out before Tim could continue.

He looked around, trying to understand what was going on, and realized he'd already been in a similar situation. The last time it happened, they'd been at the office, and ghosts had surrounded them. From the reaction of the psychics in the room, Tim suspected the same was happening now.

But these ghosts didn't stay silent and still. Tim didn't need to be a psychic to see the result of their presence in the room. The stuff on the table — notebooks, pens, mugs, bottles of water, and even cell phones — lifted in the air. Several people scrambled to grab them, and Tim did the same to his computer, which was in front of him. If the ghosts were going to throw things around, he didn't want them to break his computer.

He held it close to his chest and retreated away from the table, pressing his back against the wall. He briefly wondered if he'd passed through a ghost to do so, but he hadn't felt anything, and he wasn't sure he wanted to know.

"What's going on?" Jerome asked.

"Ghosts," Victor said. He sounded grim.

"What are they doing?"

Tim snorted without meaning to. "What do you think they're doing? Causing trouble."

Jerome's eyes narrowed, but he didn't snap at him. "You think they're doing this on purpose?"

A flying mug almost crashed against Jerome's head. He ducked just in time, and it shattered against the wall behind him, showering him with coffee. Luckily, it didn't seem hot, because Jerome's only reaction was to scowl in the direction from which the mug had come.

"This is what Curt wants, isn't it?" Tim asked. A pen hit his forehead, but he had no idea where it had come from. "He wants to use ghosts to take over the world, or something like that. It would make sense for him to use them to spy on us and try to stop us."

Jerome grunted and grabbed a notebook that flew at his face. "Does he think this will be enough to stop us?"

"I don't know what he thinks, and honestly, I don't care. I just want this to end." These ghosts had exceptional aim, and Tim had had enough of things hitting him in the forehead.

"All right," Victor's voice rose over the chaos. "Psychics, you know what to do. York, Will, and Lindsey, feel free to try to help us, but please, stay out of the way if you don't manage. I don't expect much from you, considering how little experience you have, but any help would be appreciated. Oh, and leave this gentleman be. He's Tim's grandfather."

It was hard to hear his voice over the sound of people yelping and things slamming against the walls. Tim's eyes widened when a chair started to float, but Victor's brother stepped in. Donahue gripped the chair, pulled it back down, and glared at the space where it had been floating. Nothing happened that Tim could see, but the chair landed on the floor with a loud thud. Donahue barely stopped moving. He turned his attention to another area of the room and went back to work.

Tim hated feeling helpless. He was a dragon shifter. He could defend himself and the people he cared for, but not in this situation. Right now, there was nothing he could do but wait for the psychics to be done, and he hoped it wouldn't take them long.

"How many ghosts are in the room?" he asked Will when the man rushed past him.

Will grimaced. "Trust me. You don't want to know."

Tim decided that was probably the truth. He already found it creepy that people he couldn't see were all around him.

Knowing how many there were wouldn't help.

Since there was nothing he could do, he went to the corner of the room and sat on the floor. He curled there, trying to avoid the flying objects. He thought they were slowing down, then he realized fewer objects were hitting him. A notebook still managed to smack him on the arm, and he snatched it and glared around just so that whatever ghost had hit him with it knew he was displeased.

By the time Victor and the other psychics finally relaxed, the room was a mess. Chairs had been upended. The table had been pushed to one side of the room, and it was littered with broken ceramic, dripping liquid, and pieces of paper. One of the ghosts had tried to throw a big potted plant through the window, but Elijah had intercepted it. He was still clutching it to his chest, but he put it down when he noticed that things were dying down.

Tim got to his feet. He still didn't let go of his computer, just in case, but he made his way to Victor, who was leaning against the wall and panting. The curtain of the window next to him was dragging on the floor, almost as if someone had tried to climb it.

"Are you okay?" Tim asked.

Victor nodded. "Nothing beyond a few cuts and bruises. You?"

"Same." Tim looked around the room. It seemed everyone was fine. York was bleeding from the forehead, but Leo was already on the job, fussing over him and cleaning the blood with a napkin.

"That was an experience I don't care to repeat," Elijah said. "Is this what I have to expect, working with you people?"

"I'm sure we can find somewhere else to meet," Tim said. He rubbed the back of his head where something had hit him. "I'm sorry we brought all of this to your home."

Elijah waved. "It's your home, too, and besides, I want to

be part of this. I want to help."

The door slammed open, startling all of them. For a moment, Tim thought more ghosts were arriving, but instead, it was his mother. Her eyes were wide, and she was pale, but she relaxed when she saw Tim. "Good. You're here."

Tim put his computer on the table and went to her. "What's going on?"

"I just saw on the news that something's happening in the city center. It looks like shifters are attacking humans."

Victor felt sick, but he couldn't resist looking at the TV screen when Elijah turned it on. Luckily, the TV was on the wall, and no ghost had managed to pull it off.

"The situation is grim and changing every few minutes," an anchorman said.

His blond hair looked messier than usual, which Victor imagined meant that he hadn't expected to be thrown in front of a camera right this moment.

"From what we managed to find out, a small group of shifters has attacked the university. We don't have news of victims yet, but the police force is on-site and is doing everything possible to make sure every single human there makes it out unscathed."

Victor snorted. "What are the odds that the ghosts attacked us just as this happened?" he asked no one in particular.

"You think they were a distraction?" Elijah answered. "What do Curt and the others think we would have done? We wouldn't have found out about this any sooner than we have, and we can't afford to step in. Not only do we not know what's going on in detail, but we can't expose the clan."

"Not a distraction." Victor rubbed his forehead. He had the beginning of a headache, and none of this was helping. "But maybe they wanted to make sure we were busy, just in case, and if we lost people, then it would have been a happy secondary effect."

"What do you think is happening?" Tim asked as he dropped in his chair.

"Maybe shifters *are* attacking, but if that's so, I suspect they're linked to Curt. It would make sense, wouldn't it? If he wants a war between humans and shifters, he can push them toward it through the mayor, but shifters aren't stupid. They wouldn't do something like this, especially not suddenly. No, if Curt wanted something like this to happen and spark an outright war, he had to create the opportunity. I don't believe he's the only shifter involved. Surely he has help — if anything, to kidnap the humans he's been taking. Do we know what kind of shifter he is?"

Victor looked around the room, but everyone shook their head. The only one who didn't was York, and since he was the only of them who'd spent any length of time with Curt, Victor waited for him to answer.

"A cockatrice," York eventually said. His voice was so soft Victor barely heard it.

Elijah whistled. "They're rare, maybe even more so than dragons. They live in clans, but those clans are much smaller than ours. They're loyal, so if Curt has help, it has to be from other cockatrice shifters."

Victor wasn't sure what a cockatrice was, and he didn't care. He just hoped they wouldn't have to deal with an entire clan of whatever they were. Curt was more than enough.

"Come on," Tim said, knocking his shoulder against Victor.

Victor frowned. "What?"

"Let's head out. I'll give you a tour of the house."

"We should stay."

Tim gestured at the TV. "And do what? Watch that? We already know that whatever happens, it won't be good. It's no use for us to stay here and stare. There's nothing we can do."

He was right. The only thing that would happen was that it would make Victor feel helpless, but he couldn't change what was happening or the consequences it would have. "All right. Give me a tour." Victor wanted to see more of the mansion anyway, and from the looks of it, his brothers would be fine. They were talking to the people in the room as if they'd known them forever.

He couldn't begin to imagine what it was like to live in a place like this. He'd always lived in apartments since he'd left home, but even the house he'd grown up in was nothing like this place. It was a bit much, to be honest. Victor was afraid he'd bump into something and break it.

But he still followed Tim out of the conference room. The others were already cleaning things up, and while Victor should have helped, he needed a moment to breathe. He'd expected to have to face Curt and Barton's ghosts eventually, but it had taken a lot out of him.

"Were you born here?" he asked as he and Tim walked down the hallway toward the entrance.

"Yep. It's been my home since I was born."

"Isn't it strange to live with so many other people?"

Tim shrugged. "Not really. I always have, and we're not like humans. I mean, humans used to live in big families before, right? We just never stopped. We care about the clan, and we provide whatever help we can. Sometimes it's hard to have privacy, but that's what our rooms are for."

"Can I see yours?" The words were out before Victor could think better of it.

Tim eyed him. "Yeah. Are you sure?"

"I wouldn't ask if I weren't." It wasn't like anything had to happen between them, but Victor was tired.

Barton was still in his life, and there was nothing he could do about it. But he didn't have to think about his ex. He didn't have to think about anyone but Tim, and right now, that was all he wanted to do.

Tim nodded and took Victor's hand. He didn't ask if Victor was sure again or what they'd do once they reached his room. He just pulled Victor along, walking up several flights of stairs, then down hallways. Victor was pretty sure he'd get lost if he had to find his way back to the conference room, but he didn't feel frightened. Tim wouldn't leave him alone to fend for himself.

The place could have been luxuriously decorated and dripping with gold, but instead, it looked comfortable and almost homey. The floors were tiled, and the walls painted a muted brown color that went well with the deep red curtains over the windows. There were paintings on the walls and small tables and plants scattered here and there, but nothing that interested Victor more than the door Tim stopped in front of.

Tim didn't have to unlock the door. He just pushed it open, and Victor followed him in.

The first thing Victor noticed was the king-sized bed at the back of the room. On its right was a window that opened on the yard, on its left a door, maybe to the bathroom. There had to be a private bathroom, right? The bed was messy, even though someone had tried to make it. They'd just pulled up the sheets and comforter, but there was still the indent of Tim's head in the pillow on the bathroom side.

Right in front of Victor and Tim was a small sitting area. It was next to a fireplace that looked well used and consisted of a big couch, two armchairs, a coffee table, and the fluffiest carpet Victor had ever seen. He wouldn't mind rolling around on it, preferably naked. There was a stack of books on the table, along with the remote for the TV above the fireplace. Tucked in the corner of the room was a desk with three computer screens, a mess of notebooks and pens, several dirty cups, a bottle of water, and a desk lamp.

Tim toed off his shoes and rushed forward. "Sorry about the mess." He straightened the stack of books, then the blanket that lay over the back of the couch. "I should have cleaned up, but I thought you'd be staying in a guest room."

Victor took his shoes off, too, then his socks. He strode toward Tim, grinning at the feeling of the carpet on his bare feet. Then, he grabbed Tim's arm and forced him to stop fluttering around the room.

"I don't care if it's messy," he said. "It's very you."

Tim arched a brow. "You mean I'm messy?"

"No. Well, maybe. But I like your room." Victor thought he'd like it even more if they shared it and his stuff was strewn around mixed with Tim's, but he loved it like this, too.

Tim rubbed his hands on his thighs. "Okay, so this is my room. We can bring your stuff upstairs, and I'll empty part of the closet so you can settle in."

That wasn't what Victor was thinking about now. He grabbed the back of Tim's neck and pulled him close, kissing him. He wanted to forget about everything that wasn't them, everything that was outside of this room, at least for an hour. Surely, Tim could give him that.

Tim didn't hesitate to kiss Victor back. His arms wrapped around Victor's waist, and Victor relaxed. He was safe. Nothing would happen to him or Tim as long as they were in this room.

And his heart was safe, too, in Tim's hands.

Victor didn't know how long they kissed, but after a moment, it wasn't enough for him anymore. He longed to touch more of Tim and give himself to him in a way he never had, not even with Barton. It was time to let go of the fear that Tim would break his heart. Tim would never do it, not intentionally, and that was enough for Victor.

Victor pushed a hand under Tim's t-shirt. Tim shuddered and tried to push closer, but in doing so, he unbalanced them, and Victor felt himself going back. He might have fallen if Tim hadn't been strong enough to keep him up. As it was, he took a step back to steady himself, but he only managed to stumble onto a book he hadn't seen on the carpet.

"Maybe the room *is* a bit messy," he said with a chuckle.

To his surprise, Tim hauled him up. He squeaked but managed to wrap himself around Tim, who carried him away from the couch and toward the bed.

"We're going to fall," he said.

"I'm strong enough to carry you."

And he was. Victor might be slightly taller, but while Tim was on the thin side, he was a shifter, and a dragon shifter at that. His dragon's strength shone through to his human form, and he didn't even stumble as he made his way to the bed.

Once there, he tilted forward. Victor felt himself fall again, but he wasn't afraid. He bounced on the mattress, Tim's body on top of his, and kissed Tim again.

Being on the bed seemed to have given both of them the tacit authorization to get rid of as many articles of clothing as possible, as quickly as possible. Victor tugged on Tim's t-shirt, eager to get to Tim's skin, while Tim was pulling on Victor's jeans. One of Victor's rings caught on the cotton of Tim's t-shirt and tangled there, but Victor didn't care because he still managed to pull it up and off Tim's body when Tim stopped kissing him. He did so to look down at what he was doing with Victor's jeans, and he eagerly pushed them down Victor's legs.

Victor used one foot to help, freeing one leg but not the other. He didn't need it to be free, anyway, and with Tim's hand already in his underwear, he had other things to focus on.

He pushed his hands under the waistband of Tim's jeans, relieved that Tim didn't wear jeans as tight as he did—and that he didn't seem to be wearing underwear at all.

"No boxer briefs?" Victor asked.

"They're not great when you have to shift," Tim mumbled against the skin of Victor's neck.

That was a good enough explanation. Victor kind of loved it, because it meant he could get Tim naked much more easily.

Their legs tangled together and with the fabric of both their jeans. Victor extracted just one leg, and he hooked it around Tim's thigh, anchoring the two of them together. Tim's skin was hot against Victor, and his cock was hard. It leaked against Victor's stomach and jerked when Victor thrust up.

Tim buried a hand into Victor's hair and held his head still as he kissed him. They panted into each other's mouths, moving together as if they were one. Victor's t-shirt was pushed up under his armpits, and the hair on Tim's chest rubbed against his nipples, sending sparks of pleasure all the way down to Victor's cock. The way they fit together, how Tim seemed to understand what Victor needed, all of that was more arousing to Victor than the physical aspect of sex. Tim cared about him, and in the end, that was all that mattered.

Still, Victor was happy when he felt his orgasm approaching. He enjoyed frotting because of how close it made him feel to the person he was doing it with. To him, it was more intimate than many other positions, and he was glad his first time with Tim was so perfect.

Although he could have done without the jeans still tangled around his leg.

Their movements became more frantic, their kisses sloppier. Victor pressed his head hard against the pillow, letting Tim's presence envelop him into a cocoon of care, love, and lust. Tim was giving him everything he'd ever wanted, including love, and *that* was what pushed Victor over the edge. Every time Tim touched him, Victor knew he was loved.

He trembled in Tim's arms, lost in pleasure and the weight and scent of Tim. He knew he should make sure Tim came, too, but before he could find the strength to move, Tim shuddered. The space between their stomachs became slicker, warmer, and Tim slumped.

Victor held him. He was finally at peace, and it was all thanks to Tim.

"We didn't even get naked," Tim muttered.

Victor laughed. "We can do that now."

Tim propped himself up on an elbow and looked down at him "You're okay?"

"I've never felt better." And Victor truly meant it.

Tim wished things had gone differently, that they hadn't been pushed together by circumstances, but he couldn't regret being in bed with Victor. Victor felt perfect in his arms, and when he was there, Tim knew he was safe. Right now, that was all that mattered.

Tim kissed the top of Victor's head. They were both naked now, buried under the blankets. Victor snuggled closer and sighed deeply, and Tim wondered if he was thinking about what was happening in the city center right now. Tim wanted to watch the news, but he had no wish to break the moment. Besides, he'd find out eventually. Whoever had started this mess knew what they were doing, and they wouldn't stop until they had what they wanted.

There was no way Curt wasn't involved.

"I should probably go back to the motel," Victor murmured.

"I don't think any of you should go back to your motel or your apartments. It's too dangerous."

Victor propped himself up onto an elbow. "What do you mean?"

"Curt knows we're involved. He's been sending ghosts to us, which means he knows where to find us. Here, we're safe because we have numbers on our side. Between the dragon shifters and the psychics, I think we can withstand pretty much anything. But if you go out there, even with your brothers, you could be overwhelmed." And Tim couldn't even think about Victor being taken.

Victor frowned. "We can't stay here forever."

"Just for today, then. At least until whatever's happening in the city dies down. We need to know what's going on and what the consequences will be."

Victor was tense for a moment longer, but, to Tim's relief, he finally nodded and lay down again. "I just don't like being out of the loop," Victor said. "We know Curt and Barton are involved. It's not fair that people are suffering because of them."

"I'm not saying it's fair, but there's nothing we can do at the moment."

"Well, at least you're not kicking me out of bed," Victor murmured as Tim wrapped his arms around him again.

"I'm never kicking you out of my bed."

"You say that now, but you can't be sure."

Tim had to be careful. Whatever Barton had done to Victor had done a number on him. It would be so easy to send him running. Tim wanted Victor to stay by his side, possibly forever, but he wasn't an idiot. Saying that now would freak Victor out, and Tim couldn't afford for that to happen.

"You're right," he murmured. "And you can't be sure you won't hate me by the end of the month."

"I could never hate you."

"But you can't be sure," Tim pointed out, repeating Victor's words. "I know you're not ready for a relationship, and that's fine. We can take things slow, see where they go day by day."

"I feel it's not fair to you."

"You let me worry about what's fair or not fair to me. I

knew what I was getting into when I decided I wanted to be with you. I can give you all the time you need to wrap your mind around the fact that I'm not like Barton and that I'm not going to hurt you, abuse you, or do whatever he did to you."

Victor splayed a hand on Tim's chest. "I know all of that. I'm just not sure why you're taking this so easily. Most people would have already shown me the door."

"Why? Because you need time after your last boyfriend fucked you up? The people who would have already left are idiots."

Victor chuckled. "I can't say I disagree."

"I like where we are, Victor. It's much more than I expected we would have already, and I'm fine with giving you time and space to deal with your feelings and memories. I'll still be here once you're done, waiting for you. And I promise to tell you if this isn't enough for me anymore," Tim added in a rush. He could see Victor already thinking about that. "But I'm perfectly fine with what we've been doing for now."

"There could be more kisses," Victor said.

His tone was lighter, a sign Tim hoped meant he was finally allowing himself to believe that Tim was in this for the long run.

"There will be as many kisses as you want and as much sex as you're ready for. I feel like we're growing closer day by day, and like this was another step toward what we both want."

"Sex is easy," Victor murmured. He drew designs on Tim's skin with his fingers. "Feelings aren't. I know you're nothing like Barton and that you're not going to hurt me, but part of me can't help but wonder if I'm doing the right thing. When I left Barton, I thought I was leaving all chances of a relationship behind. I didn't believe I could trust anyone ever again, yet you managed to do the impossible. I want to be okay with this, but part of me is still terrified that you're going to change."

Barton had really messed Victor up, and Tim wanted to go out there, find him, and let him know what he thought of that. "That's what he did?" he asked instead. "He changed when you started dating him?"

"Well, he was always a bit of an ass. I don't know why I didn't see it sooner, but I suppose I was young and in awe. But yes. He was different at the beginning of our relationship. I think that once he realized I wasn't going anywhere, he allowed his true self to show. That's when I knew I'd made a mistake, but I still stayed with him." Victor softly snorted. "I thought I could change him or something stupid like that. I believed that no one else would want me, and that surely I was in the wrong and the problem in our relationship was me, not him."

"I'm glad you finally realized that wasn't so."

"Me, too, and I wish I never had to see Barton again."

"One day, you won't have to."

"But until then, he's still in my life."

"Not because you want him to be, and things are different now. You're fighting against him, and you're not letting him deceive and hurt you. We can do this, Victor. We'll find out what he and Curt are up to, and we'll put an end to it."

"The problem is that I'm not sure it'll be enough to stop Barton. Even if we stop whatever they're doing, he's not going to get arrested. His brother won't allow that to happen."

Tim wouldn't mind killing the guy, but he didn't want to scare Victor. Besides, he was pretty sure that if he found himself in front of Barton, he wouldn't be able to go through with it. He wasn't a fighter. He was a computer nerd, and no matter how strongly he felt about Victor, he didn't think he could spill blood.

Or maybe he could. He supposed if someone threatened the people he loved, including Victor, he wouldn't hesitate to hurt them. Did that make him a bad guy? He didn't think so. He'd hand over Barton, Curt, and whoever was working with them to justice if he could. In this situation, though, he doubted the system would help. If the mayor and the chief of police were in this up to their necks, they'd no doubt make sure they didn't pay for what they were doing.

They'd have to pay in a different way, and at the moment, Tim didn't see death as the worst option.

CHAPTER EIGHT

Victor might have moved to a new motel, but that didn't mean he liked the new place any more than he'd liked the old one. He itched to go back to Tim, but once the mess in the city center had blown over yesterday, he and his brothers, along with Gunter and everyone else, had headed out. There was safety in numbers, but they couldn't avoid going home. Tim had offered for Victor to stay at the mansion and share his room, but Victor had refused.

He wanted to say yes. When he was with Tim, everything was easier. Even thinking about Barton was. Tim was showing Victor that he wasn't like Barton and that Victor didn't have anything to fear from his ex-boyfriend, and it wasn't something Victor had expected or thought he'd ever have. But with Tim, he felt he had a new beginning, a chance at a fresh start, and he didn't want to mess things up. Tim said he didn't mind waiting, and Victor didn't want to fuck things up by rushing into this. He knew he wasn't making a mistake, but he wanted to ensure Tim wasn't.

Victor disliked quietness, so he turned on the TV. He wasn't surprised to see the news anchorman was talking about what had happened yesterday. No one knew what had started the fight, but some people said they'd seen shifters trying to kidnap humans. They'd stepped in to stop that, and the fight started. The shifters had fled without taking the humans, and things would have been fine if they'd stopped there.

The problem was that they hadn't.

For most of the night, people had been protesting and

hunting shifters. Victor felt better knowing that Tim was safe behind the mansion's walls, but Tim wasn't the only person Victor worried about. Between his brothers, the clan, and everyone else, he had many people he cared about, and he was terrified of losing any one of them.

Victor took his phone from the bed and pulled up Tim's number. He wanted to make sure Tim was safe at the mansion and to hear Tim's voice.

"Hey," Tim said when he answered. "I was just about to call you."

Victor found himself smiling. Now that he was with Tim, he was smiling more than he ever had before. He was pretty sure his brothers had already noticed and would soon say something about it, but between the meeting yesterday, the mess with the ghosts, then the fights in the city center, they hadn't had the time to talk yet.

"Were you?"

"Yeah. Elijah asked me to."

Victor blinked. "Elijah? That's not what I was expecting to hear."

Tim chuckled. "Sorry."

"Don't be. Just tell me what's going on."

"You've seen the news?"

"Is there anyone in the city who hasn't?"

"I suppose you're right. I'm worried about you and your brothers out there, and so is Elijah. We had a clan meeting, and he asked everyone what they would think of opening the mansion to you and the others. If you stayed with us, we'd be sure you're fine."

"You want us to move in with you?"

"Wouldn't that be the easiest way to make sure everyone is okay? You'd all be safe here."

"For now, only shifters are in danger," Victor pointed out.

"For now. Look, I know you're hesitant about our

relationship, and that's fine. You don't have to stay with me in my room if you don't want to. We have plenty of guest rooms, and you can either have one to yourself or share with your brothers. We're afraid that after shifters, psychics and mages will be attacked. Besides, even if that doesn't happen, Barton knows you're involved. He or Curt could send someone to hurt you, even though you're not a shifter."

Victor had just been thinking that he didn't feel safe in his motel room and that he wanted his family to be protected. It would be hypocritical of him not to agree to this. Besides, he doubted his brothers would want to move into the mansion if he wasn't with them.

They were annoying that way.

"Have you already called the others?"

"Not yet. I'm not the only one making the phone calls, though. Leo has already contacted Marcel and Will, and I'm sure Jerome and Lindsey will find out about this soon. Elijah said he was calling Gunter, although he didn't look hopeful that Gunter would agree."

They barely knew Gunter, but then Victor supposed the others barely knew his brothers. Yet the dragons were opening their mansion, their *home*, to them. Victor was humbled by the trust they were putting in them, and he hoped no one would break it.

"I'll call my brothers. It would be easier for them to say yes if I'm the one asking them."

"Good. Does that mean you're coming?"

A flash on the TV made Victor look in its direction. The mayor was on screen, looking like he was about to give another press conference. "What the fuck?"

"The mayor," Tim said grimly. "I'm watching TV, too."

Victor turned the volume higher.

"After what happened yesterday, we can't afford things to continue the way they are," the mayor said. "We're still not sure what happened, but we can't allow violence to be used by either side."

Victor snorted. "He's really saying shifters are at fault as much as the humans who attacked them?"

"Are you surprised?"

"Not one bit."

The mayor was still talking, so Victor turned his attention back to him. "I'm creating a curfew for shifters. Until we know what's going on and that they're not involved, they won't be allowed to be away from their homes after seven in the evening. This is for protection, both theirs and the people who live in the city."

Victor swore. "Really? For fuck's sake. Why is the curfew limited to shifters?"

The mayor paused, then continued, "I'm also forbidding for groups of shifters to meet. Families can stay together, but beyond that, shifters aren't allowed to be in more than groups of three."

"What about clans and packs?" Victor asked. "Does he consider them family?"

"I don't think so," Tim said. "I wouldn't be surprised if eventually, someone came knocking on our door demanding we disband."

"What's going to happen then?"

"They won't like what happens. The clan is our home, and we'll do everything we have to in order to keep our family safe. If it means an outright war against the mayor, that's what the mayor will get."

Victor swallowed. He understood where Tim was coming from, and he couldn't say he disagreed, but it was too easy to imagine what a war between dragons and humans would mean. The clan was numerous enough that if most of the members decided to step into the fight, it wouldn't end well for humans. The problem was that it wouldn't end well for the clan, either. They were bound to lose dragons, and everyone would be hurt if that happened.

Victor prayed things wouldn't come to this.

"I need you to come to the mansion as soon as possible," Tim said.

His voice was more serious, and if Victor had been tempted to say no before, he would've changed his mind now. He had no intention of staying at the motel. By going to the mansion, he'd be safe, and he'd be able to keep an eye on both his brothers and Tim.

"I'll call my brothers as soon as I hang up with you, and we'll head to the mansion once we're packed. Stay safe, Tim."

"I should be the one telling you that. I'm in the mansion, safe and sound, but you're out there. I'm tempted to come to pick you up."

"Don't." It was impossible for a human to identify a shifter by sight, but Victor didn't want to risk anyone recognizing Tim. "We'll be fine. We'll be out of the rooms and into our cars. Give us half an hour, and we'll be home."

"I'll be waiting for you."

"You won't have to wait long."

"Get me more clean sheets," Tim's mother snapped at him.

Tim gave her a little salute and disappeared into the hallway. That was where the spare sheets were kept for the guest rooms, and he was lucky enough to snatch the last pair. He carried them back to her, and she went to work changing the sheets.

The old ones weren't dirty, but they'd been on the bed for a while now, and she wanted to wash them. Tim understood, but with so many people temporarily moving in, he wasn't sure they could afford not to have enough clean bedsheets.

"They're going to have to share," he said.

"Hopefully, some of them won't mind. They're brothers, right?"

"Some of them. Others are couples, so it shouldn't be a problem." Tim doubted Jerome would want Lindsey out of his sight. He didn't fully trust the clan, but then Jerome didn't trust anyone except Lindsey and possibly Will.

"Your cousin is bringing his boyfriend?"

"Both of them are. They wouldn't leave Will and Lindsey on their own."

Tim's mother nodded. "Good. That way, I'll finally meet them. Are they ashamed of their family? I know Will because he's Jerome's best friend, but I haven't seen him since he and Marcel got together."

Tim wasn't touching that with a ten-foot pole. "You'll have to ask them, but I don't think so. Neither of them has been with their boyfriends for long, and with everything that's been happening, I don't think they've had time to think about introducing them to the family." Did Will need to be introduced again anyway?

Tim's mother didn't look convinced. "You've met them."

"Because I work with them. I promise Jerome and Marcel didn't mean anything by not bringing them around sooner. Besides, you'll see them now, right?"

She nodded and went back to work. Tim tried to help her, but she waved him away.

"Go and check if everything else is ready."

"As long as you're sure you don't need me."

"I don't. I want everything to be perfect for our guests."

Tim almost told her it wasn't necessary, but she wasn't fretting over so many people moving in with them. She was terrified that something would happen to Tim and his father, or any other dragon shifter in their family. She was human, and she probably felt like she couldn't do anything. She wasn't wrong, but Tim was a dragon shifter, and he couldn't do anything, either.

When the doorbell rang, Tim was more than happy to rush toward the entrance. By the time he got to the front door, the gate had been opened, and several cars drove in. He recognized Victor's, so he went toward that one as they started parking. He was by Victor's side as soon as Victor was out of the car, and they fell into each other's arms.

Tim hadn't realized how worried he was until now, but he could finally relax with Victor in his arms safe and sound.

"I was worried," he confessed.

"I was worried, too, even though I knew you were safe here. I think everyone is having trouble right now," Victor said.

"We're getting guest rooms ready, but some of you will have to share." Tim hesitated. This might be pushing too much, but he wouldn't know until he tried. "You could stay in my room. I can sleep on the couch if you're not comfortable sharing a bed with me." Although Tim hoped Victor would be.

He wanted what they'd shared yesterday to become a common occurrence. He wanted them to go to sleep together and wake up together, but he wasn't sure Victor was ready. Everything had gone so slowly initially, but now it felt like they were rushing a bit, and not just because they wanted to. If it hadn't been necessary, Victor wouldn't be moving into the mansion, so there wouldn't be a question over whether or not they should share a bed.

But Victor patted Tim's chest with a smile. "Your bed is more than big enough for both of us."

"As long as you don't feel I'm pushing you into something you're not ready for."

"That's not what I'm worried about. To be honest, you and our families are the only things keeping me from panicking. I can't help but wonder what Barton, Curt, and the others are doing. We thought they were kidnapping humans and using their life energy, but what's going on with these attacks? Why did the mayor create a curfew and all those rules?"

Tim didn't have an answer. He'd been thinking about it, though, and he suspected he wasn't the only one. He wrapped an arm around Victor's waist and didn't let him go even as Victor reached into his car to grab his bag.

"I think they knew someone would finally notice the many humans disappearing, and they needed to provide an explanation."

Victor nodded, and they walked inside, followed by the others. Tim guided everyone to the living room, where it would be easier to gather and get everyone's attention. Several people were there, probably curious about their new guests, but to Tim's surprise, they didn't turn to watch them. Instead, their attention was riveted on the TV, and he groaned when he saw the mayor was on the screen once again.

"For fuck's sake," Tim said. "Doesn't the man have something more important to do than give press conferences?"

Victor put down his bag and put his arms around him. "He's trying to move the attention from what he and the others are doing to the humans they're kidnapping. If he manages that, they'll be able to keep going, and the city will end up in a war. If he wants to take over, he needs to get rid of powerful shifters who might stop him."

Like the clan.

Tim's stomach churned. Was Curt planning to attack the clan? He didn't have an answer, and he wouldn't get one anytime soon, so he turned his attention to the TV.

"Everything is going well. There haven't been any more attacks on humans, and we've arrested two people involved in what happened yesterday. I don't want anyone to worry. Our police force is working hard to find the missing people, and I'm sure they will soon. It's important to keep the peace, though, so I ask all shifters to please follow the rules that have been put in place. They're there to keep both humans and shifters safe."

Tim snorted. Did anyone believe the guy? Did he even believe himself? Tim didn't need to be a genius to see that the new rules had been set up to repress shifters. It gave the humans the upper hand, and if shifters tried to fight back, the mayor would be able to point at the rules they'd broken.

It was a shit show, and it was about to get worse.

He gasped as a big group of people on the screen took out signs that put them firmly on the shifters' side. He understood their frustration and anger, but was the mayor's press conference really the best place and time for this kind of protest? Tim could have predicted it would be a disaster, and he'd have been right. Almost as soon as the people — shifters, possibly — raised their voices, humans started pushing them around and insulting them. Tim couldn't do anything from where he was except watch as the protest turned into a fight. Shifters were strong, but there were so many more humans that they didn't stand a chance.

One of the shifters turned into a lion and roared. A few humans scattered, but not enough, and the others threw themselves at the lion. Tim squeezed his eyes shut when he saw an arm being torn from the body it belonged to. The screams buried themselves into his brain, and he knew he'd have nightmares for days, possibly longer.

"They're doing exactly what Curt and the mayor want them to do," Victor whispered. His focus was on the TV, and he looked horrified, just as much as Tim felt.

"They're showing everyone that we *are* the monsters the mayor has been pointing out for his crimes," Jerome said grimly. Tim hadn't even noticed he was in the room.

He was right. The shifters were only defending themselves, but they were doing so in their animal form. They were showing everyone watching the press conference that they weren't fully human and wouldn't hesitate to hurt humans. Yes, it was in self-defense, but most people wouldn't care about that. They would only care that shifters had hurt humans, and they would act accordingly.

CHAPTER NINE

All of it felt like a dream, and not a pleasant one. Victor wished he could go back home to the clan, bury himself into the bed he shared with Tim, and never come out. Instead, he was in the middle of a crowd he felt was about to attack him.

Tim hadn't wanted Victor here, and Victor hadn't wanted Tim to be present. That meant both of them were there, along with the rest of the psychics, Gunter, and most of the dragon shifters who'd wanted to help. This could end in a shit show, and Victor still wasn't sure it was the best idea, but while the dragons had listened to what he had to say, they'd decided against his opinion.

He understood why. They'd been hiding in the mansion for more than a week, and tension was running high. They all knew it was a temporary fix and that eventually, the humans would attack. That was why Elijah had decided it would be better for them to take the first step, and Victor hoped he wasn't wrong.

There had been protest after protest over the past week. The first fight between shifters and humans, during the press conference, had resulted in the deaths of one shifter and three humans. More humans were in the hospital, and while Victor was sure shifters were, too, they were never mentioned. Humans had won that fight, but one would never believe it, looking at the news.

And the mayor kept having his fucking press conferences. Every day, he was on the TV, saying nothing about the investigation but insinuating that shifters were involved and that humans should take matters into their own hands and do something about it. More protests had started all over the city, but this was the biggest one yet.

Victor and the others were here because they wanted to make sure things wouldn't degenerate. Victor and the other psychics were keeping an eye open for ghosts while the dragons tried keeping other shifters away. This was a human protest against shifters, and the humans were angry. Victor had never seen anything like this, and even though he was human, he was terrified.

He doubted the people around them would care what he was or wasn't. If they wanted to kill him, they would, and he was starting to realize that the shifter thing was just an excuse. The mayor was using it to appeal to what humans felt, and in most cases, it was fear and distrust of shifters. Now that humans didn't have to be civil anymore, they were attacking shifters, and it wouldn't end well for anyone.

This would be the perfect situation for Curt to use his ghosts. Even if no shifter intervened during the protest, ghosts could be enough to create the illusion of it. The fights would get worse, and the city would truly tumble into war.

Victor felt like he was living in a bad movie, and he didn't know how to get out of it. He wasn't even sure he could.

Tim's grandfather suddenly appeared next to Victor, startling him. Victor glared at Kenneth, but he couldn't talk to him openly without attracting attention, so he took out his phone, made sure the ringer was off so it wouldn't start ringing, and raised it to his ear. "Have you found anything?" he asked.

Victor had found out what Kenneth had been doing when he wasn't with Tim. He'd been surprised to see the ghost wasn't around Tim a lot, especially after Kenneth had said he found his nephew entertaining. Then Kenneth had explained that he'd been hanging around the ghosts who'd appeared in the break room at Jerome and Will's office. He'd followed them after they'd left and infiltrated their ranks. That meant he was right in the middle of things, and he was able to come and go and tell Victor what Curt was doing.

They'd been right. Curt was using his girlfriend and other mages and psychics to suck out the life energy from the humans he was kidnapping. Some of their bodies had started appearing, and of course, shifters had been blamed for their deaths.

"Yes," Kenneth said. From his expression, Victor could tell it wasn't good.

"What's going on?"

"They're going to use the protest. The ghosts have orders to keep as many humans as possible here. Curt is going to use his mages and psychics to suck as much life energy from them as he can, then to take their blood."

Victor felt sick. "The life energy he gets from the people he kidnaps isn't enough anymore," he murmured.

Kenneth nodded. "I heard him say it's too slow going and not enough. That's why he wants to use the humans here."

Curt could get the life energy of thousands of people at the same time. He didn't care if he killed them. Hell, it was probably a plus if he managed to do so. He could suck every single crumb of life energy from the humans around him, and, considering how angry they were, it would be a lot. Then these people would die, and the mayor would blame shifters. The rest of the city would only see what they wanted to see, and more shifters would be hurt.

"We have to stop it," Victor murmured.

"How?" Kenneth asked.

Unfortunately, Victor didn't have an answer. "We have to find Curt and his mages. Stopping them is the only way to stop all of this. Can you tell me where they are?"

"I can take you there, but are you sure it's a good idea?"

Victor wasn't sure of anything except for the fact that he had to do something before the people on the street died.

Tim wished he could be anywhere but here. He didn't like the mass of people around him, knowing what he did about them. They wouldn't hesitate to kill him if they found out he was a dragon shifter, and now he understood better why Victor hadn't wanted him and the others to come.

He was still glad he was here.

The fact that he wasn't with Victor made him nervous, but at least he was close by. If something happened to Victor, Tim would be able to step in and protect him. He didn't care if he had to shift and expose himself as a shifter. He was a dragon, and he'd stomp all over the people who tried to hurt the man he loved.

His phone vibrated in his pocket, and he slid it out. They'd all agreed to communicate through texts so no one would overhear anything. Victor was convinced Curt and Barton would use this opportunity to do something, and Tim agreed. He just didn't know what they do, but Victor might have found out.

Talked to Kenneth. Curt is going to use his mages and psychics to pull the life energy from all the humans present here today. He'll raise his ghosts, and it'll kill them.

For one second, Tim was breathless. There had to be thousands of people around him. Could Curt really get life energy from all these people? Was it wishful thinking on his part, or did he have a plan?

Knowing him, he probably did. Tim wasn't sure it was a good plan, but they'd apparently reached the moment in which Curt stopped caring about what happened to the city. Besides, he'd probably find a way to blame all of this on shifters, even though they couldn't have taken anyone's life energy even if they'd wanted to. This was the work of mages and psychics, but humans wouldn't realize that. The people present today were so angry at shifters that they didn't care about the truth. They just wanted their pound of flesh, and they wanted it now.

Is that even possible? someone asked in the group text.

Gunter's name appeared on the screen. *I don't think it's ever been done before, but it's certainly possible in theory,* he wrote. *It depends on how many psychics and mages Curt has working for him. And that's not the only thing he can do with so many humans.*

Tim didn't really want to know, but he still found himself texting, *What else can he do?*

I've been thinking about it, and he would be stupid if, after killing so many people, he didn't also use their blood. Or maybe that's why he's here? He'd need psychics to suck the life energy from so many people, but if he already has enough of that to control and strengthen a number of ghosts, he could use the ghosts to kill people and then use their blood.

Tim didn't want to find out any more details about this, but they had to know, didn't they? *What do you mean?*

Curt could use the blood to bolster whatever spell he's using to gather ghosts and make them more powerful. He wouldn't even need the blood of everyone here. If he did manage to use all of the humans present, though, it would be the most powerful blood spell ever used.

And that's bad? Lindsey asked.

It's very bad, Gunter confirmed. *If that's what Curt is planning, we have to stop him. He could flatten the entire city to the ground if he had that much power.*

How does blood give power? Tim asked.

It's similar to life energy, Gunter told him and everyone else in the group chat. *Without blood, you die. It gives you life, and it's powerful if you know how to use it.*

How would he go about getting the blood from all these people? It's not like you can ask them to stick out their arm, Tim pointed out.

No, but he can use a spell. If he's already sucking the life energy from these people, they're going to get weaker and weaker. It wouldn't be hard for him to use another spell to make them even more compliant, then kill them. He doesn't need to take the blood in a particular kind of way. He just needs to kill them and make sure they have an open wound.

And he'll blame shifters for it.

Probably.

There was no *probably* about it. If Curt managed to do this, he'd point the finger at shifters, or rather, his friends, the mayor and the chief of police would. Then it would truly be hunting season on shifters in the city, and no one could afford for that to happen. Besides, they couldn't let all these people die. Tim couldn't say he liked them very much, considering everything, but he also didn't want people to die. They were being manipulated by Curt, Barton, the police chief, and the mayor, and they didn't know any better.

In a way, it would be the truth, one of Victor's brothers typed in the group text. *Curt is a shifter, so it would be a shifter's fault.*

Tim scowled at the screen. *What side are you on?*

I don't want these people to die. I was just pointing out that maybe if we manage to expose him, it would make things easier on the rest of the shifters who live in the city. Maybe we can show everyone that only one shifter was involved.

That wasn't a bad idea, but Tim wasn't sure it would be enough. There was no other way out of this, though. Whatever happened next, they had to save the people gathered here to protest having shifters living in the city. They wanted shifters to be kicked out, and instead, shifters would save them.

Tim would make sure of it.

He looked around. No one was paying attention to him, which was good, considering he'd spent the past ten minutes texting. He was supposed to be careful and keep his eyes open, for fuck's sake. *How do we know who works for Curt and his friends in this crowd?*

We don't, Victor answered. Tim was relieved to see his name on the screen because he'd been quiet, and it made Tim worry. *Assume every human you don't know works for them.*

Tim almost groaned. *That's hundreds of them.*

Plus the ghosts. He can use people's blood to control them, and he doesn't have to kill anyone for that.

Great. So Tim and everyone else were surrounded by enemies. It wasn't anything new, but these people might be even more dangerous than Tim had initially assumed. *How do we stop Curt?* he asked.

For a moment, no one answered. Tim could imagine they were thinking about what to say, but he didn't know any more than any of them. Then Victor's name appeared on his screen again.

We need to find Curt.

That was what Tim had been afraid of.

CHAPTER TEN

"Kenneth, I need you to find Curt," Victor said, raising his phone to his ear.

Kenneth nodded. "I'll go, but will you be okay?"

"I don't think anyone will be okay until we stop Curt and his friends, but I'm as fine as I can be, considering the circumstances."

Kenneth nodded. "I don't want anything to happen to you. My grandson loves you."

That made Victor blink. He and Tim were together, but they hadn't said those three words yet. "He certainly likes me," he said.

Kenneth shook his head. "Trust me. I've been watching my grandson since he was a child. He loves you, and I don't want anything to happen to you. It would kill him."

"I can't make any promises, but I'll do my best not to get killed."

Kenneth nodded. "You do that. I'll go find Curt so we can finally put an end to this madness." He vanished, and Victor lowered his phone. He looked around, trying to think like Barton. He'd never met Curt, so maybe he couldn't think like him, but there had to be a way for him to find out where Curt was.

It had to be a place that made sense for Curt's plans. He needed easy access to the people on the street, which meant he was probably around here somewhere.

But where?

Victor looked around. The street was full of people talking, screaming, and waving signs that told shifters to leave the city and go home. It didn't matter to these people that the shifters who lived here *were* home.

Victor understood where their fear came from. Shifters were not just different, they were also stronger. After what had happened during the press conference, humans were very much aware of what would happen to them if they got into a fight with a shifter. There was strength in their number, which was probably why so many of them were here today. They were being manipulated by people who should have their back, and they couldn't even see it.

But none of that mattered. If they attacked, Victor would do everything he had to in order to defend Tim and the rest of their friends. He wouldn't allow anyone to get hurt, especially not because of Curt.

He looked around again. He clutched his phone, terrified he might be about to get a text or a call that someone was in trouble. For now, everything seemed to be normal, but Victor suspected it wouldn't last long. Whatever Curt was planning, it was about to happen.

For some reason, there was a stage built against the buildings on one side of the street. It wasn't big, but it made it look as if someone would give a speech. It would be exactly like the mayor to do something like that and try to make the crowd even angrier.

Victor almost dismissed it, but something behind the stage caught his attention. There were people there, setting things up, and Curt stood in the middle of them.

York had done a pretty good job describing him and his girlfriend. Victor knew it was them even from a distance, and he took a step forward before thinking better of it. He raised his phone, quickly texting the group to let them know he'd found their enemies, then he started moving again.

His phone vibrated in his hand. He tried not to let it distract him because he needed to get to the stage, but the crowd didn't make it easy on him. It was almost impossible to move without stepping on feet and bumping into people, and even though Victor apologized, he still made several people angry. He thought one guy was going to punch him, but he managed to wiggle his way away from him and disappear into the crowd again.

He finally reached the side of the street. He wasn't close to the stage yet, but at least from here, it would be a straight line, and he'd be able to stick close to the walls. He looked at his phone again, mostly because it kept vibrating and making him anxious. He didn't read all the texts that arrived while he was walking, sticking to the last few instead.

Everyone, head to the stage, Elijah ordered.

We're trying, but it's impossible to get there quickly with so many people here, Donahue answered.

We have to be fast, Victor quickly typed. *Whatever Curt is planning, he won't wait until we reach him. He's going to act, and he'll do it soon.* Victor squinted, trying to see what Curt was doing. *His girlfriend is with him, and she's not the only one. They're talking, but she has stuff set up in front of her on a table.*

They're starting the spell, Gunter said. *We need to stop them.*

Victor stared at the space between him and the stage. How was he supposed to do that?

His phone vibrated again, causing him to look down. His eyes widened when he saw Tim's words.

I'll create a distraction. You get to Curt.

Victor started typing a reply, telling Tim not to do something stupid, but he didn't have the time to send the text. Tim's distraction became obvious when people suddenly started screaming and a huge dragon grew from somewhere in the crowd.

Victor had never seen Tim's dragon form. He'd wanted to, but he hadn't even thought to ask with everything happening. They'd have time once Curt had been dealt with, and he wished that was how things had happened rather than how they were happening now.

Tim had shifted in the middle of the crowd. Victor knew he'd have been careful not to hurt anyone, but with so many people crowding the street and his dragon form being so big, he was bound to have broken a few limbs.

Victor's heart raced. He was beautiful, with the light glinting off his turquoise skin. Victor wasn't afraid of him, but he could see that others were. People were screaming and trying to run, while others were attempting to get to Tim, no doubt to hurt him. A guy pushed past Victor, a gun in his hand, and Victor didn't hesitate. He grabbed the guy's arm, turned him around, and punched him in the face.

Pain flashed in his hand, but that didn't stop him from punching the guy again. The guy fell back, his eyes wide in surprise, and was carried away by the fleeing crowd. It was only one man, but at least he wouldn't start shooting at Tim.

Victor desperately wanted to go to Tim, but it wouldn't do any good if they didn't stop Curt. He was closer to the stage now, and he could see that Curt and his girlfriend were working with the stuff they'd put on a table in front of them. They were about to cast their spell, and Victor couldn't allow that to happen.

So instead of following his heart and pushing his way to Tim, he went the other way. As long as he kept close to the wall, he managed to wade through the crowd. It was thinning, but not quickly enough that Curt wouldn't be able to hurt people if he cast his spell now.

Something hit Victor's back, propelling him forward. He went down on one knee and was pushed down again when he tried getting back to his feet. He couldn't allow the crowd to get him all the way to the ground because it was too easy to imagine what would happen then. The crowd would run him over, and he'd probably die.

A hand grabbed his arm and pulled him up. He tried twisting around to thank whoever had saved him, expecting one of his friends, but the words stuck in his throat when he found himself face to face with Barton.

"What are you doing here, Victor?" Barton asked.

He was alone, but somehow, the crowd wasn't getting close to him. It was as if he was surrounded by an invisible wall — except it wasn't invisible to Victor, who could clearly see the ghosts.

"I could ask the same of you," Victor said.

Barton shook his head. "Unless you're here to tell me you've decided to join Curt and me, it was a very bad idea to come."

Victor had to agree with him on that.

Okay, maybe shifting in the middle of a crowd who hated shifters hadn't been Tim's smartest idea. As it was, he didn't have a way to leave. He could fly away, but he needed to stick around and help the others deal with Curt and Barton. If he stayed and shifted back, everyone would know he was a shifter because he'd be naked.

What was he supposed to do now?

Someone punched him in the side. It barely tickled, but he still twisted his big head around to glare at the human. The man squeaked, then, unless Tim was mistaken, peed his pants. The stench of urine was obvious even in the crowd, and he wrinkled his nose.

For some reason, that scared the guy even more.

Tim huffed, and a plume of smoke escaped his nostrils. He didn't want to stay here with so many humans around, but since he couldn't leave, he hopped up onto a car, trying to put more distance between himself and the humans. He extended his wings, trying to find Victor in the crowd. It was impossible to see anything, though. Some of the humans had picked up trash and were throwing it at him, which kind of made him want to roar at them. The problem was that he didn't want to act like those humans thought he would because he was a shifter. It had been bad enough when the lion shifter had torn apart the humans who'd attacked him.

Tim noticed someone waving at him. Marcel stood in front of a shop, holding a bundle of clothes in his arms. When he realized he had Tim's attention, he gestured behind himself. Tim hoped he understood correctly, and he rose higher in the air, intent on flying over the building and landing behind it. The humans under him cried out, but he ignored them.

The alley at the back of the building was too tight for him to land there in his dragon form. He eyed the ground, know-ing he'd have to shift and land midflight. He stretched his wings one last time and shifted.

It was more of a jump than he'd expected, and it jarred his legs when he landed. He rolled, tucking himself into a ball, cringing at the thought of what he was landing on. He was naked, and here he was, rolling around the trash in the back alley of a shop.

"What the fuck were you thinking?" a harsh voice asked. A hand grabbed his arm and pulled him to his feet, and he found himself staring into Jerome's eyes.

"Now isn't the time to scold him," Marcel said. He was there, too, and he thrust the bundle of clothes he was holding into Tim's arms. "Dress, and be quick. I'm sure the humans are already looking for you."

Tim obeyed. He'd lost his phone in the crowd, and he doubted he'd find it again, but that was okay. He could get a new one. What he couldn't get a new one of was Victor, and as soon as he was dressed, he turned to his cousins. "Have you seen Victor?"

Marcel's expression was dire. "He's behind the stage with

Curt and Barton."

Tim swore and started running. He ignored Jerome and Marcel calling for him. Was Barton hurting Victor? The man didn't even need to hit him to hurt him. A few well-placed words, and Victor's heart would crumble.

Just the thought made Tim want to smash Barton's face into the ground.

There were fewer humans on the streets now. A lot of them had run away when he shifted, and while Tim would never have hurt any of them, it was one of the things he'd been aiming for. He'd wanted to give his friend a distraction and to get as many humans as possible away from Curt.

The problem was that there were still plenty of humans hanging around, looking for the dragon. They didn't seem to realize he'd already shifted back, and they barely gave him a second glance when he ran past the crowd. He didn't hesitate, didn't stop, just rushed toward the stage. He was almost there when Gunter suddenly appeared in front of him. Tim tried to go around him, but Gunter grabbed his arm and shook his head. He pulled Tim forward, and since Tim wanted to go to the stage anyway, he followed. But Gunter didn't let him go to Victor, even though they could see him now. Instead, he tightened his hold on to Tim and kept him back.

"I need to get to him," Tim whispered harshly.

"I know. But we have to be careful. What's going to happen if you barge over there?"

Tim looked around Gunter to the situation he'd be barging toward.

Curt and Barton stood next to a table. The blonde woman next to Curt had to be his girlfriend, the psychic mage. She was doing something in a bowl, and when she took a step back, Tim's stomach churned at the sight of the red liquid in the bowl. It had to be blood, which was a sign that Curt had already started whatever he was planning.

Something pressed against Tim's side, and he turned to see that Gunter had taken out his phone and was recording the scene in front of them. Tim's instinct was to go to Victor, who was clearly unhappy to be by Barton's side. Victor wouldn't want him to do something stupid, though—or rather, something even more stupid than shifting in a crowd of humans who hated shifters.

"Why the fuck is he here?" Curt snapped.

Curt had to be in his late forties, possibly early fifties. His hair was still dark, with silver strands highlighting its darkness. His eyes looked like they were about to start shooting lightning bolts at Barton, but Barton didn't appear to care. Curt's cheeks were flushed, and he towered over Barton, but he was almost the same height as Victor.

"What did you expect me to do?" Barton asked. "Leave him out there to die?"

"You gave him a chance to join us. He refused, so his place is there. What did you think would happen when you dragged him here?"

Barton shook his head. "No. I'll convince him to come back to our side. I won't let you kill him and use his blood for your ghosts."

Curt hissed. "Shut your mouth. Someone could be around here, listening to us."

Tim sucked in a breath and pulled Gunter deeper into the darkness under the stage. He didn't think Curt had seen them, but he didn't want to risk it.

"Who cares if someone can hear what we're saying?" Barton asked. "They're all going to die soon anyway."

"Are you really going to kill all these people?" Victor asked.

"We need them to die," Barton answered.

"Why? What are you trying to obtain from this? I know Curt wants to raise an army of ghosts, but what are *you* gaining from it?"

"Money," Barton said. "I'll have so much money that I can buy you whatever you want."

Victor shook his head. "I don't want anything from you. I'm not here to join you, but rather to stop you."

Barton laughed. "How are you going to do that? They've already started the spell, and soon the ghosts will rise. With the life energy we stole from the humans we kidnapped, they'll have enough power to kill everyone left on the street. Then Curt can use the blood for his blood spell."

Gunter sucked in a breath.

Gunter had mentioned blood spells the few times, but he'd never gone into details, and Tim didn't want to know any because he'd heard enough. He just needed to know what to do to stop the spell from happening.

"What blood spell?" Victor asked.

"It'll give the ghosts strength, enough that we can take over the city."

That was all Barton managed to get out before Curt hit him in the face. Barton stumbled back, his eyes wide.

"Shut the fuck up," Curt snapped. "What do you think, that you're a villain in a stupid movie?"

"He's not going to tell anyone."

Curt turned his attention to Victor. "You're right. He's not because I'm going to kill him." He raised his arm, hitting Victor like he had with Barton. He must've put more force into it, because Victor cried out.

That was all Tim could take. With a roar, he shifted again, exploding the clothes Marcel had given him earlier. His form was too big for the stage he and Gunter had been hiding under, and it broke down, pieces flying everywhere. Tim's only focus was Curt, though, and he dove toward him just as he started shifting.

For a moment, Victor had no idea what was happening. His cheek hurt, but it wasn't the first time someone had hit him, and unless he was lucky, it wouldn't be the last. It wasn't enough to put him down, and he grabbed the corner of the table, trying to keep his balance.

He was just in time to see Curt shift.

York had told them that Curt was a cockatrice shifter, but Victor had no idea what that was. The only thing he knew was that cockatrice shifters were even rarer than dragons, which would explain why most people didn't know what it was.

He wished he'd never found out.

He realized that most cockatrice shifters were probably nice people, but that didn't make them any less ugly. Curt looked like a dragon had mated with a chicken, and the cockatrice was the result of that unholy union. Curt had wings like dragons, but his face and neck were feathered. The feathers faded on his body and wings, which were leathery. Instead of a mouth with fangs, he had a beak, and a forked tongue came out when he roared.

Even the roar was different. It was squeakier, but it was no less intimidating, considering what Victor was looking at.

Curt stood up on his back legs. He didn't have front legs like dragons, and instead, he used his wings to help him rush toward Tim. There was nothing Victor could do for Tim, and trying to step into the fight would only distract him. Hopefully, the other dragon shifters in the crowd had seen what was going on, and they were coming to help.

No, there was nothing Victor could do to help Tim, but there *was* something he could do to stop Barton.

His ex stood there with his eyes wide as he took in the fight. He wasn't holding Victor anymore, and Victor placed himself in front of him. "What the fuck were you thinking? You were ready to kill people to get money and power? I always knew you were an asshole, but I didn't realize just how bad a person you were."

Barton didn't seem offended by Victor's words. "What would I care about these people? You saw how easily they were manipulated into believing shifters were behind this. They're idiots, and they don't deserve to live. Come with me, Victor. I promise I won't kill anyone, and we can get back together and use Curt's money to run. We can be happy away from the city."

Victor wasn't surprised Barton was still trying to convince him to get back with him. Barton probably couldn't understand why Victor wouldn't want to. He'd always been vain, and somehow he still believed that Victor was here because he wanted them to get back together, not because he wanted to stop him.

"We can go wherever you want. Curt never mattered, and I don't care about his plans. I don't care that he wants an army to take over the world. I just care about the money he gave me, and we can use that money to get whatever we want. We'll be far away from him, and he won't be able to hurt us."

"But you'll allow him to hurt these people?"

Barton waved. "They don't matter, Victor. They're ready to hurt people who had nothing to do with this just because they're afraid. Blaming shifters wouldn't have worked if they hadn't been prejudiced assholes, and you know that. Most humans will never accept shifters, just like they won't accept us. We're different. We're *better*, and humans can't wrap their minds around that."

"You think you're better than humans? You're not, Barton. If anything, you're worse. You're a spoiled brat who's always been given everything he wanted, but I won't allow you to do the same this time. You're going to pay for what you did."

Barton blinked as if he didn't quite understand what Victor was saying. That didn't last long, unfortunately. His expression turned angry, and he took a step toward Victor. "I won't allow anyone to stop me, not even you. If you're not coming with me, step aside, or I'll hurt you."

Victor stood his ground. "I'm not going anywhere, and neither are you."

Barton cried out and threw himself at Victor. They'd never physically fought, and Victor hadn't thought Barton would ever do something like this. He wasn't prepared when Barton's body barreled into his, and they both hit the ground. The air whooshed out of Victor's lungs, and before he could take another breath, Barton hit him.

It hurt. Curt's earlier punch had hurt, but Curt had put more force behind it. Maybe it was because Barton still thought of Victor as someone he loved, or maybe it was because Barton wasn't trained. Whatever the reason, it was easy enough for Victor to grab Barton's wrist and wrench it aside when Barton tried punching him again.

They rolled on the ground, hitting the feet and legs of the people fighting around them, but Victor couldn't pull his attention away from Barton. He had to believe the others had finally stepped in and that they were making sure no one would get hurt. Victor's entire focus needed to be on Barton. He wouldn't allow his ex to run away. For the first time ever, Barton would face the consequences of his actions.

"We could have had everything we wanted," Barton said as he grabbed Victor's head and slammed it against the ground.

Victor saw stars. He gripped Barton's wrists, trying to push him away, but he was at a disadvantage in this position. Barton managed to slam Victor's head into the ground one more time before Victor dislodged him. They rolled, and this time, Barton ended up on the bottom.

Victor's head hurt. He could feel blood trickling down his neck, and he'd be surprised if he didn't have a concussion. He pinned Barton's wrists to the ground, using all his weight, and kept his ex there. Barton struggled, but he wasn't going anywhere as long as Victor stood strong.

"Let me go!" Barton screamed. "My brother is going to kill you. He'll make it look like an accident or a suicide. Your parents and brothers will think you killed yourself, and they'll never find out the truth. They'll hate you."

Victor didn't care what Barton was saying. He'd won, and Barton wasn't going anywhere.

A loud crash and a roar of pain made Victor turn around to check in on Tim, and that was when Barton struck again. He hit Victor's jaw, pushing him back. Victor rolled and hit his head against the ground, which didn't help his shaky vision. He scrambled to grab the knife Tim had given him. He hadn't wanted it, but Tim had said he'd feel better if he knew Victor had it, so he'd taken it. Victor had promised himself he wouldn't use it, but at this second, he realized it was either that or being killed by Barton.

He wouldn't allow Barton to do that to him. Barton wouldn't win, not this time.

Barton screeched and threw himself at Victor. His expensive clothes were torn and dirty, and he had blood dripping from his nose. His gaze was wild, and Victor briefly wondered if Barton was even rational right now. He didn't look like it, but he appeared ready to kill Victor, and Victor was ready to defend himself.

The knife felt heavy in his hand. Barton landed on top of Victor, and, as soon as he had Victor pinned under him, he wrapped his hands around Victor's neck. This time, Victor couldn't buck him off, no matter how hard he tried. Barton slammed Victor's head against the ground a few times, and his fingers tightened around Victor's neck. Victor's vision was turning black, and he did the only thing he could do.

He raised the hand in which he was holding the knife, and

he sank it into Barton's side.

Tim threw himself in Victor's direction. He'd seen Barton trying to strangle Victor, and now that the others had arrived and were fighting with Curt, he could step away from that fight and protect Victor.

He wasn't sure what happened, but before he could reach Victor, he saw Barton flop onto his side. There was blood coming from his stomach, and when Victor sat up, Tim saw the knife in his hand. Victor scrambled away from Barton's body, and Tim shifted as he reached him, wrapping his arms around him. Victor yelped and tried stepping away, but he relaxed and threw himself into Tim's arms when he realized it was Tim. The knife clattered on the ground, and Tim buried his face against Victor's neck.

"Are you all right?" Tim needed to know

There was blood dripping down the back of Victor's neck, and when Victor reached for his head, he winced. "I'm pretty sure that's going to need stitches," he said.

Tim wanted to kill Barton with his own hands and to make him hurt for what he'd done to Victor, but when he looked at the man, he realized he wouldn't need to.

Barton was on his back, blood seeping out of the wound on his side. His shirt had been white once, but now it was streaked with dirt and plastered to his side, the bloodstain getting bigger as the seconds passed. Barton pressed a hand against his side, but from what Tim could see, it wasn't doing him any good.

"I need a hospital," Barton said. "Victor, call my brother. Tell him to get me."

Victor hesitated. Tim suspected he didn't want Barton to die, but he'd done what he needed to do to protect himself. Tim kept an arm around Victor's shoulders, holding him close.

"He won't make it," he murmured.

Victor's dark eyes were wide. "How can you be sure? Maybe an ambulance could get here in time."

"Look at how much blood he's losing. I don't know what you hit when you stabbed him, but I'm pretty sure it's vital. Even if we can get an ambulance here, he won't make it to the hospital in time."

Victor slumped against Tim's side. "I didn't mean to kill him."

"I know. You did what you had to do. Don't feel guilty."

"We could have been so good together," Barton said. His words were slurred now, a sure sign he was about to lose consciousness. "You ruined everything. Why did you ruin everything, Victor?"

"I couldn't allow you to hurt so many people," Victor whispered.

"We could have had everything," Barton repeated.

Then he stopped breathing. His eyes stared at the sky, but he clearly wasn't seeing anything anymore. He was dead, and as far as Tim was concerned, that was the best outcome. He just wished Victor hadn't been the one to kill Barton — Victor would blame himself for the rest of his life.

Victor sobbed once and turned into Tim's arms. He buried his face against Tim's neck, and Tim held him, silently telling him he'd be here for him, whatever happened.

They didn't have time to waste, though, and as soon as Victor had gathered himself, they both turned toward the fight happening behind them.

Curt was surrounded. He'd shifted back, and one of his arms looked like it was broken. He still stood defiant, completely naked, his pale skin streaked with dirt and blood, several long cuts marring his chest, stomach, and face.

"None of this matters," he declared. "Everyone who was

here today saw the dragon shift. They'll know it was shifters who did this. They'll kill all of you."

"Not once I publish the video I took of you and Barton talking about your plans," Gunter said. He stepped forward, his phone in his hand. He pressed a few things on the screen, and Barton's voice came out loud and clear, explaining what Curt's plan had been and that he'd manipulated humans to believe shifters were responsible for the disappearances of their loved ones.

Curt paled and looked around. He was surrounded, and even if he shifted back, there was nothing he could do. Tim was in his human form, but Jerome had shifted and looked ready to tear off Curt's head if he got close enough. Elijah was in his dragon form, too, as was Leo. Even if Curt tried flying away, the dragons would stop him.

"This isn't over," he said through gritted teeth.

"It looks to me like it is," Marcel said, stepping forward. "Give up, Curt. You won't ever take over the city, the country, or the world. Shifters are not better than humans. We're just different, and you need to accept that."

Curt stood up straighter. "You and the humans you seem to love so much will pay for everything you've done," he said.

His voice was stronger, and Tim *knew* he had something up his sleeve. Sure enough, objects scattered around them started moving. Victor sucked in a breath, and someone cried out, "Ghosts!"

Then everything turned to chaos. Tim twisted, shielding Victor with his body and letting whatever the ghosts were throwing pelt his back, but Victor pushed him away. "We have to repel the ghosts," he said as a chair flew over his head.

Tim knew he was right, but he was still terrified. "I'm staying with you."

Thankfully, Victor didn't say no. Instead, he turned, focusing on a spot where Tim couldn't see anything, and started working.

He wasn't the only one. The other psychics in their group were doing the same, each of them protected by a dragon. Tim saw Curt's girlfriend rush to him and drag him away, but he couldn't abandon Victor. It was obvious from the way he moved that he was fighting many ghosts, possibly too many for him to repel, and Tim would never forgive himself if something happened to Victor and he wasn't here to protect him. All of them wanted to stop Curt, but protecting the people they loved was more important. They'd get Curt the next time he tried something stupid.

And he would. Tim was sure of that.

Tim didn't know how long it would take Victor and the others to repel the ghosts. Things around them, from chairs to tables, and even a car, were being thrown at them by invisible hands. Tim wasn't sure how many ghosts had to work together to pick that car up, but he was glad when it slammed back on the ground without hurting anyone, making the ground shake under Tim's feet.

Tim looked around. There was nothing he could do to help the psychics, but he'd make sure no one came close to Victor. They hadn't obtained the result they'd been aiming for, and Curt was in the wind again, but not everything was lost. They had Gunter's video, and hopefully, that would help smooth things out between humans and shifters. The relationship between the two groups would never be a great one, but Tim was fine with that as long as no one tried to kill each other just because of what they were.

He had no doubt that Curt would eventually try something else. The man was bitter, and he thought he deserved more than what he had. But Barton was dead, and Tim hoped that meant the mayor and the chief of police wouldn't continue working with Curt. Even if they did, Curt would have to lie low for a while, and it would give everyone time to heal and be on their guard.

It took much longer than he'd expected for the ghosts to finally vanish. He couldn't see them, but he thought he felt the moment when the last ghost was finally gone. For a second, nothing and no one around him moved. They were all suspended, waiting for the ghosts to do something else, but they never did.

"They're gone," Victor said in a trembling voice.

Then he tilted sideways, and Tim barely had time to catch him before he hit the ground.

CHAPTER ELEVEN

"We still don't know who the shifters were," the anchorwoman said.

Victor was doing his best not to stare at the TV. He supposed he could ask for it to be turned off, but everyone wanted to find out what the humans knew about what happened during the protest. Several dragon shifters had been seen, along with a strange shifter Victor now knew was a cockatrice. It was important they keep an eye on what the humans were doing, just in case they found out who the dragons were and decided to do something about it.

But having the TV on meant that Victor had to listen to stuff about Barton several times a day, from how he was a loving brother — lie — to how he'd been misguided and influenced by Curt and wouldn't have done this if it weren't for the cockatrice shifter — also a lie.

"The chief of police announced that his brother's funeral would be closed to the public. This morning, he gave a press conference, promising to find the people who killed his brother." The anchorwoman was going through all the information she had at the moment, apparently. "The investigation is ongoing there, too."

"Everything okay?" Olsen asked as he sat on the couch next to Victor.

Victor almost screamed when his brother startled him. He'd been on pins and needles since the fight, and he wasn't sure if it was because of the fight itself or of what he'd done during it.

He'd killed a man.

He knew that if he hadn't killed Barton, Barton would have killed him. He could still feel Barton's hands around his neck, and every night, he woke up feeling like he couldn't breathe. Even though Barton had claimed he loved him, he wouldn't have hesitated to kill Victor if it meant getting away with what he was doing. The only person who'd ever been important to Barton was Barton himself, no matter what he claimed.

There would have been no other way out of the situation, but that didn't mean Victor had an easy time accepting what had happened. He didn't know if he'd ever be able to or if he'd ever stopped thinking about Barton. Hopefully, he would at least stop having nightmares, because he needed sleep.

"Victor?" Olsen asked, leaning closer.

He looked worried, and Victor didn't blame him. He plastered a smile on his face, but he doubted he was fooling anyone, especially one of his brothers. They'd grown up together, and they knew when Victor was full of shit.

Maybe he should talk to someone. Tim had been tiptoeing around him as if he was afraid Victor would break if he mentioned anything about the fight, and considering how he was behaving, Victor didn't blame him. His brothers hadn't pushed, either, but they knew Victor much better than Tim, and eventually, they would.

The fact that they all decided to stay here at the clan wouldn't help Victor avoid them. Curt was still out there, licking his wounds and probably thinking about what he'd do next, and they'd all decided it would be safer if they continued living together. It wasn't a hardship, anyway. The mansion was massive, so they each had more than enough space not to bother each other. Donahue had made noise about bringing his cat over since, for now, the cat was still with their parents, but he hadn't left the house yet.

They were safe here, and if Victor had a choice, he'd never leave. He realized it was trauma talking and that eventually, he'd have to face what he'd done. Curt wasn't going to lie low for long, and when he rose again, Victor would be there to stop him, along with the others.

That was why it was important for Victor to make his peace with what he'd done.

He forced himself to smile at his brother. "I'm fine."

Olsen stared at him for a moment. Victor could almost tell what his brother was thinking, so he wasn't surprised when Olsen snorted.

"That's bullshit, but I'll let it go. You'll be fine eventually, though."

Victor found himself smiling. "You sound sure of that."

"That's because I am. I know you feel horrible because you killed Barton, and I'm not going to tell you he was a fucking asshole and that I'm glad he's the one who died rather than you."

Except he just had, but Victor stayed silent.

"That's how I feel, though," Olsen continued. "It's how we all feel. I know it doesn't help because you still killed him, but he *would* have killed you if you hadn't."

"I know."

"Do you, really? Because you loved him once. It's not just that you killed a man. It's also that you killed someone you cared about for so long."

Victor leaned the back of his head against the couch and stared at the ceiling. "I haven't loved him for a long time. Honestly, I'm not sure I ever did. I loved the idea of him, the version of himself he showed me, and what he promised. I loved what we could have in the future, but now I realize we would never have had it. Barton was selfish and cruel. He was abusive, even though he never hit me. I wish I hadn't had to kill him, but I don't feel guilty for saving myself."

"You still feel guilty for killing him, though."

Victor looked down at his hands. "I'm just not sure how to deal with it. I have nightmares, and I can still feel the blade sinking into his side."

Olsen patted Victor's knee. "I'm really sorry about all of this. I wish I could do more to help you, but I don't know how."

"You don't have to help me. Like you said, I'll heal eventually. In the meantime, I'll have to learn to live with the nightmares. Besides, I'm sure I'm not the only one having them."

Olsen sighed. "Probably not."

This time, Victor was almost relieved when he saw the mayor's face appear on the screen. He already knew that whatever he was about to say wouldn't be good for him, but neither the mayor nor the chief of police knew he had anything to do with his brother's death. No one knew he did. They were looking for the killer, but the protest had been a complete mess.

With Gunter's video, they hadn't been able to continue insisting that shifters were behind all of this. Barton had admitted in front of everyone that he was the one behind this, along with Curt. Of course, Curt was a shifter, so in a way, the mayor had been right, but now people knew that not all shifters were evil. They really should've known that before, but Victor supposed it was better late than never.

"Our search for the man who was behind the kidnappings is ongoing," the mayor said. "We can't share any more information, but be assured that we *will* find him, and he'll pay for what he did. As many of you know, Barton was one of my best friends, and I won't allow his killer to walk free."

Hopefully, the mayor truly believed that Curt was behind Barton's death. It would be one less thing for Victor to worry about, and while he hated the thought of someone paying for something he'd done, Curt wasn't innocent. If he ended up behind bars, he'd have earned it.

Victor supposed he had, too. It had been to defend himself, but he'd still killed someone.

The couch dipped on Victor's other side, and he turned to see who it was. He wasn't surprised to see Tim smiling at him, and when Tim held out his hand, Victor took it. He linked their fingers together, needing Tim's strength as he watched the mayor talk about how many victims from the protest were still in the hospital and how many of them had finally gone home. Many humans had been injured, but as far as Victor was concerned, the city was safe, at least for now.

"They don't know it was you," Tim whispered.

Victor nodded. "I know. I'm not afraid they'll find me."

"Good, because I wouldn't let them touch you even if they did."

Tim was fiercely protective, even more so after what happened during the protest. It was like he was afraid Victor was going to break down, and Victor couldn't deny that sometimes he felt like he would. If he did, though, Tim would catch him. He wouldn't be the only one, either. The people around Victor cared about him, and it didn't matter to them that he'd killed a man. Hell, Leo had seemed oddly impressed by what Victor had done.

"But we now know that the community of shifters in the city had nothing to do with the disappearances," the mayor continued.

Victor could tell he was pissed, although he suspected he was one of the few who could. He was glad he hadn't made enemies out of the mayor and the chief of police, although he doubted they'd be nice to him if they ever met again. As long as they didn't try to kill him, he was fine with that. He wouldn't be nice to them if he met them, either.

"No matter how much I cared about Barton, I can't deny

what he said in that recording. He was working with someone, had been influenced by him, and while he died, we're still looking for the shifter responsible for all of this. That and the ongoing investigation into Barton's death are what we're focusing on right now, and of course, on making sure the families of the people who'd been taken know what happened to their loved ones."

Victor's throat closed off. When he thought about all these people who had died, he wanted to cry, even though he couldn't have helped them any more than he had. Only some of them had been found, and all had been dead. Victor wasn't surprised, but he still wished he'd been able to do more.

He suspected that was how he'd feel about this for a long time. No matter how hard he'd tried, he hadn't been enough. He was going to have to live with that for the rest of his life, and he wasn't sure how.

Was Tim overreacting by keeping an eye on Victor? He didn't think so. It wasn't just Barton's death that Victor had taken hard, but also the fact that they hadn't been able to save any of the people who'd been kidnapped. Not everyone had been found, but what were the odds that the people who hadn't been were still alive?

As the mayor droned on, making everything about himself and what he'd lost, Tim kept an eye on Victor. He was staring at the screen, but his expression was smooth. Actually, he didn't have an expression. He was just staring, and if Tim hadn't known him as well as he did, he might have missed the pain in Victor's eyes. But it was there, and Tim wished he could take it away.

But he couldn't. Victor would have to learn to live with what he'd done and what they hadn't been able to do. The same went for all of them. It was sad that they hadn't been able to save the humans who'd been taken, but at least they'd stopped Curt and Barton. Surely that had to amount to something?

Of course, Curt was still out there. Tim had no doubt that eventually he'd come back. He thought he deserved so much more than what he had, and he was going to get it, no matter what he had to do to obtain it. He hadn't hesitated to use shifters, then humans. Curt didn't care about people. He only cared about himself and what he felt he was owed, and that was dangerous. It was especially dangerous because Curt knew who they were and that they'd been involved. Tim had no doubt he'd use that knowledge eventually.

But for now, they were safe. They were home at the mansion, and everyone was sticking around. The fight wasn't over, and they'd be ready when Curt reappeared.

Tim wasn't surprised at how much he enjoyed living with Victor and the others. Jerome had been grumbling about needing his own space and his apartment, but he hadn't made a move to go home, probably because of Lindsey. He wanted his boyfriend to be safe, and there was no safer place than the mansion.

Marcel was happier than his brother to be living with the clan, and he and Will had brought along Will's cat. Apparently, one of Victor's brothers had a cat, too, and he'd been making noises about bringing it as well. Elijah had said it wasn't a problem, and since Tim knew how important it was for Victor to have his brothers safe and close, he hoped they'd settle down.

It was a lot of people to take in at once for the clan, but the clan had always been messy. Having these people living with them wouldn't change that, but it would mean they were safe, which in the end, was all that mattered.

They didn't just have to look out for Curt. The mayor and the chief of police had been involved, and they'd lost Barton.

They'd do what they could to make whoever had killed Barton pay, and unfortunately, that person was Victor. Tim had never liked the mayor, but he disliked him even more now. He'd make sure to vote for his opponent the next time there were elections, but hopefully, it wouldn't take that long to get the guy to resign. He had to pay for what he'd done eventually, right?

"I just wanted to make sure everyone here has everything they need since you've moved in," Elijah said as he rose to his feet. "I know this isn't an easy situation, and of course, none of you are forced to stay with us."

"But you still think it would be safest," Donahue yelled from the other side of the living room.

It was a tight fit, and Tim made a mental note to check with Elijah whether they should buy more couches.

"I do. Curt is still out there, and he knows we're involved now. He's seen several of us, and while I can't be sure he knows you and your brothers are part of this, he certainly knew about Victor. Do you want to risk it?"

Donahue looked at Victor and shook his head. "No. Besides, this is great. It's like being a teenager again. I even have to share the bathroom with my brother."

"At least I don't leave dirty socks all over the floor," Roslin pointed out.

Elijah cleared his throat and glared at the two of them. "As I was saying. You're welcome to stay for as long as you want and to settle down. I know some of you have been sharing the guest rooms, and if you want, we can find a way to make it work so that each of you has a personal bedroom. It's going to take some thinking and reorganizing, and we'll have to redecorate and fix some of the rooms, but I want all of you to feel like you're home here and have your private space. Living with so many people, especially dragons, can be a lot."

Tim knocked his shoulder against Victor's. "So you and

your brothers are staying, right?"

"I already told you we were," Victor answered with a smile.

"Does that mean you're officially moving in with me?" Victor had been staying in Tim's bedroom since he'd arrived, and Tim wouldn't have wanted it any other way. It wasn't good enough for him that Victor was in the mansion. He wanted Victor as close as possible, as often as possible, and living with him was the best way to obtain that.

"I thought I already had," Victor pointed out.

Tim grinned and kissed Victor's temple. "I guess you have. I'm glad you're staying."

Victor leaned against Tim's side, and Tim wrapped an arm around his shoulders. He loved that Victor was easy with his affection. "I wouldn't have it any other way. Besides, I was kind of tired of all the motels."

"So you're using me for my mansion."

"Exactly. For your mansion, but also for your body and your huge heart."

Olsen, who was sitting on Victor's other side, groaned. "Can we not talk about Tim's body? Not all of us are having regular sex."

Victor grimaced. "Can we not talk about sex? You're my brother."

"You started it."

"I didn't say anything about sex. I just mentioned Tim's body."

"And we all know what you do with his body."

Tim snickered. It wouldn't be easy to find a way for all of them to fit together, but in the end, they were family. It wasn't a family most humans would have understood, but these humans did. Their clan was big and messy, but the most important thing was love, and they had plenty of that. They cared about each other, even about the newest additions, and they'd need that love to face the fight that was coming for them.

Because it was. Curt was still out there, and he wouldn't stop until he died or he got what he wanted. Tim would make sure he never did, which meant one of the people in this room right now would eventually kill Curt.

Looking around, he couldn't help but wonder who it would be. It didn't really matter, though. As long as Curt couldn't hurt anyone else ever again, Tim didn't care what happened to him.

EPILOGUE

Victor hated watching the news. Every time he turned on the TV, it was to hear Barton's name or see the mayor talking about how his best friend had been brainwashed. Nothing could be further from the truth, but the mayor would never admit that, and Victor didn't expect him to.

But there was something worse. A bunch of bodies had been found in the river, most of them belonging to the people who'd disappeared. Curt was cleaning house, starting with the humans he'd kidnapped.

They'd been drained of blood. Victor had somehow expected it, but it still shocked him. He wasn't a mage, and he didn't know much about blood magic, but from the way Gunter talked about it, it was clear it wasn't something most people would dare use. It wasn't hard to believe Curt would do something like that. He'd taken not only those people's life energy, but also their blood. He'd wanted everything they could give him, and killing them hadn't been a problem for him.

Victor hated that all these people had died, but he supposed that at least their families knew what had happened to them. The chief of police had declared that Curt had been behind this, although no one knew why he'd done it, and Victor doubted anyone would find out. There was no proof that the mayor and the chief of police had been involved, but Barton never did anything without talking to them. When Barton was involved, they were, too, and Victor would prove that. He didn't want Curt to hurt anyone else, just like he didn't want the mayor and the chief of police to do the same.

The problem was how powerful they were. He couldn't get to them, and he couldn't do anything unless he found definitive proof they were involved.

But the fight wasn't over. Whether they'd fight only against Curt or also against the mayor and the chief of police, Victor didn't know, but he suspected they'd find out soon enough. At the moment, everything was quiet, and he'd been training York, Will, and Lindsey. Whatever happened next, they needed to know how to deal with ghosts.

"It's a fucking mess," Gunter muttered over his breakfast.

Victor flipped the bacon in the pan before turning to him. Gunter was staring at the TV screen, his mouth full, and he looked pissed.

"Do we know who Curt's girlfriend is?" Victor asked.

Gunter blinked. "What do you mean?"

"Well, I don't know much about mages, but psychics aren't really common. Usually, if we've lived in a place long enough, we know everyone in our community, even if it's only from a distance. Does the same go for mages?"

Gunter stared. "You mean I should know her?"

"No, but maybe that someone you know does. I don't know how much good it would do for us, but it would be a place to start. Curt is dangerous, and he's definitely behind all of this, but what about his girlfriend? Curt can't do magic, just like he can't deal with ghosts. His girlfriend does both those things, though, and maybe it's time we focus on her." As much as Victor didn't want to focus on any of this, they had to. Curt wouldn't be gone for long when he'd decided that the city and the people who lived here owed him.

Gunter pointed at Victor with his fork. "You know, that's not a bad idea. I should've thought about it sooner."

"It's been a mess lately. I'm not surprised you didn't."

Gunter scowled. "I still can't believe I have to live with

these fucking dragons."

"You say that only because of what happened yesterday."

Gunter bared his teeth. "Damn right. I can't believe they threw me in the pool."

Victor had to suppress a smile. He'd been there yesterday when a few of the younger dragons in the clan had been playing around. It had ended with Gunter in the pool, still clothed. The dragons had found it hilarious, but Gunter less so, although Victor suspected that he wasn't as angry about it as he was behaving. Gunter was having a hard time getting used to living with so many people, but the same could be said of the others.

Jerome especially was snarky about living here, even though technically, he belonged more than Victor. He was a dragon shifter, and his family was part of this clan. Still, he continued bitching about having to share his living spaces, but everyone was used to it by now.

"I'll contact some friends," Gunter said. "Someone has to know who she is. Even if she arrived in town with Curt and was never seen here before, they've been here for a while. She's bound to need some ingredients for her magic, at the very least. Someone has to be aware of her presence, and maybe they know where she's hiding."

"It might not lead to anything, but it could also help us get rid of both her and Curt, so I guess it would be worth it."

"Exactly. You're a genius."

Victor shook his head. "Not a genius. I've just been obsessing over this for way too long."

That was what Victor did when he couldn't sleep at night, and unfortunately, it happened way too often. He didn't usually have any problems falling asleep, mostly because he tired himself out as much as he could during the day. He hoped it would help with the nightmares, but it didn't. When he woke up during the night, breathless and feeling like hands were still squeezing his throat, he started thinking. He needed to make sure Curt paid for what he'd done and for that to happen as soon as possible. He felt it would be easier for him to leave the past behind if Curt weren't hiding somewhere, plotting their demise — possibly while twirling his mustache or something like that.

"Is that bacon I smell?" Tim asked as he walked into the kitchen. His hair was still messy from sleep, and it made him look adorable.

Not that he needed help in that department. Tim was always adorable, but especially so when he just woke up.

He stopped next to Victor, wrapping an arm around Victor's waist, and leaned in to kiss Victor's cheek.

"You weren't next to me when I woke up."

Victor kissed him back, but quickly because he didn't want to burn the bacon. "I didn't want to wake you up. You went to bed late last night."

Victor wasn't the only one still working to find Curt and his girlfriend. Many of the people in the clan were, including Tim. He'd been digging into the mayor's and the police chief's personal files. It was illegal, but by this point, no one cared. They just wanted to find proof that they'd been involved and possibly use that proof against them so they couldn't hurt anyone ever again. They might not have been involved in the killings or even in life energy and blood thefts, but they'd still known what was going on. They'd blamed all of it on shifters, had used it to get rid of people they didn't like, and that just wasn't right.

But it was slow going. Victor had no doubt that they'd find something soon enough, but in the meantime, they had to wait.

That was always the worst part.

"Is that bacon for me?" Tim asked.

He wrinkled his nose as he made a show of sniffing the air,

which shouldn't have been as adorable as it was. Tim was a grown adult, a fierce dragon shifter, yet Victor's heart skipped a beat every time he saw him.

He'd never thought he'd have this again when he'd left Barton. Now, he realized he'd never actually had it. His relationship with Barton hadn't been a relationship at all. Barton had manipulated and used him, but things couldn't have been more different with Tim. Tim truly cared about Victor, and Victor loved him.

He pressed his body close to Tim, burying his face against Tim's hair. "You can have all the bacon you want. I love you."

"That's — thank you. I'll take the bacon." Victor could hear the smile in Tim's voice. "I love you, too."

Victor would fight to preserve this. Now more than ever, he had people to fight for.

He wouldn't disappoint them.

ABOUT THE AUTHOR

Catherine is the creator of several series, most of them paranormal, including the Whitedell Pride Series and the Gillham Pack Series. While she graduated in translation, she decided to go the writer's way because it was more fun to create her own stories and characters.

She's been living in Italy for more than twenty years, but she's a daughter of the North — Belgium to be precise — and she misses it so much that she's already planning to move back.

She loves pizza — probably too much — her son, her pets, and of course, books. She sneaks some reading time into her schedule every time she has five minutes free from writing, demands from her various pets and son, and lastly, housework.

Connect with her:

lievens.catherine@gmail.com
BookBub: https://www.bookbub.com/authors/catherine-lievens
Website: https://authorcatherinelievens.com/
Facebook: https://www.facebook.com/catherine.lievens.9
Facebook Group: https://www.facebook.com/groups/411788002341528/
Twitter: https://twitter.com/authorCLievens
Newsletter: http://eepurl.com/c-uvKn

www.ingramcontent.com/pod-product-compliance
Lightning Source LLC
Chambersburg PA
CBHW060824120626
46557CB00001B/351